Watch for a TALL WHITE SAIL

By MARGARET E. BELL

"One of the best 'young novels' to be presented for many a day."—*Saturday Review of Literature.*

The seacoast of Alaska is the background for this story of young love and heroic endurance. It was in 1887, from the deck of the northbound steamer, that sixteen-year-old Florence Monroe first saw the tall white sail. She and her family were being transplanted from their home in Victoria to Alaska, where her father had started a salmon-fishing business. Florence's part in the venture was to go to the lonely fishery at Nichols Bay to keep house for her brothers. It was

(*continued on back flap*)

grief are met with courage and enriched by a delicately handled romance."—*New York Times*

"An extraordinarily fine book. Written with skillful style and fast pace, this story carries a ring of truth."—*Allied Youth*

"The reading of this book is a vital experience."—*San Francisco News*

Watch for a TALL WHITE SAIL

ALSO BY *Margaret E. Bell*

THE PIRATES OF ICY STRAIT

DANGER ON OLD BALDY

ENEMIES IN ICY STRAIT

WATCH FOR
a Tall White Sail

A NOVEL BY

Margaret E. Bell

Frontispiece by LOUIS DARLING

WILLIAM MORROW AND COMPANY

NEW YORK, 1948

Seventeenth Printing, September, 1971

Printed in the United States of America.
Published simultaneously in Canada.

to Florence Millar

Watch for a TALL WHITE SAIL

CHAPTER 1

Thick-maned work horses were dragging the last empty drays up the wharf, their heavy hoofs beating a hollow thud on the wet planks. Stevedores were loading the last freight into slings, and the ship's boom swung out, dangling a great iron hook over their heads. The air was filled with the sound of men's voices, the clank and rattle of loading gear, and occasional bursts of raucous laughter. Beyond the wharf, the houses and stores of Seattle looked raw and new among the stumps of a hillside denuded of its forest. In 1887 it still wore the vigorous, challenging look of the pioneer city.

The steamer lying at the dock was alive with the activity of departure. Black smoke boiled out of the stack into the rain; mail for the towns of Southeastern Alaska was brought on board; passengers mounted the steep gangplank and disappeared into companionways. On the wharf men stood waiting: loggers, mill hands, Indians, fishermen, and a group of Seattle's lumbermen and merchants. On the decks of the steamer there were drummers going north to get orders for merchandise; some of them would stay and become merchants, themselves. There were trappers, prospectors, gamblers, miners, and members of whaling and fishing firms. There were no women.

On the other side of the dock the Canadian sidewheeler from Victoria, British Columbia, had let off passengers and lay idly waiting. The purser of the American boat came briskly down the gangplank carrying a closed umbrella in his hand. He hurried through the rain and boarded the Canadian vessel, entering the saloon through a door near the head of the plank. A moment later he emerged with a lady in plum-colored traveling costume on his arm. He opened the big black umbrella and held it over her as he assisted her down the gangplank. A tall, slender girl followed them, and behind her was a young man to whose hand a little girl clung. Last of all came a gray-eyed boy with a basket. Heads turned as the purser led the group across the wharf.

The girl, Florence Monroe, stepped gingerly among the puddles on the wharf. In one hand she clutched the long skirts of her traveling costume, pulling them to one side just below the small conservative bustle. In her other tightly gloved hand she held a large umbrella carefully, in order not to disturb the taffeta ribbon that rose in blue loops from the middle of her new bonnet. Her dark auburn hair was brushed up smoothly at the back, leaving a little tendril or two curling at her neck. On this rainy June day she had turned sixteen and she was wearing her first real lady's clothes. She was about to spend the first night of her life away from home. In her grave, young face her hazel eyes were unhappy and distraught.

The Monroe family were being transplanted. Early that morning they had closed the door of their big home in Victoria. They had gone through the garden and closed the gate, not looking back where they knew Ma's rosebush over the door was covered with June buds. In the carriage Florence had sat very straight, looking over the quiet, familiar town for the last time. As they drove down the hill her face had been strained and severe from her effort not to cry. Already it seemed ages and ages ago.

This steamer, toward which she was going now, would take them from Seattle to a place called Wrangell, in Alaska. Pa and the two older boys were to meet them there; it was to be the end of the second lap of their journey. She hadn't seen Pa and Alexander and Gregory for two years. For two years she had known that this was going to happen but, somehow, it hadn't seemed real until now. Pa's new salmon-fishing business was established, his new home was built, and he had his own boat to take them from Wrangell to his place at Klinkwan on Prince of Wales Island. That was a name one would expect to find in Canada and it had a familiar and comforting sound. But to Florence, Alaska meant wilderness. In his letters Pa had said it was a "wee bit o' Scotland, bluebells and all." To him it was a land of opportunity—a new world.

But Florence liked the old world: Victoria and home and friends. She felt uncertain and a little frightened now that the first lap of the journey was behind them. Every now and again she glanced up at Ma's little plum-colored back being steered through the crowd of bewhiskered men by the purser of the American boat. He had met them, as Pa's letter had said he would, and now he was doing his best to keep the umbrella from dripping into the pink roses on Ma's bonnet. Little Ma walked briskly along, holding her skirt up out of the puddles and talking brightly to the purser. As they approached the steep gangplank, men moved aside to make room for the ladies, and Florence felt her face flush under the stare of their curious eyes. She felt uprooted and strange and woe-begone.

Close behind her came Jaimy, her twin brother, tall and big-shouldered for his age, looking even bigger than he was as he guided their little sister Laura up the wet gangplank. Laura was only ten, and she was excited and thrilled to be traveling. Her red-gold curls bobbed up and down as she skipped along, peeking from under her umbrella in an effort to see everything. Their brother Roderick brought up the rear carrying the Monroe cat, McDuff, in a covered hamper. Roderick was thirteen, and he was taking in every bit of the activity of the wharf. He paused on the gangplank to look over the heads of the men, past the stern of the steamer to where a tall-masted sloop went tacking across the wind on the gray water of the bay.

On the rain-spattered deck the air was full of the smell of cigar smoke and wet wool. The purser was talking to Ma. "Mr. Monroe is fine, ma'am, just fine. We saw him on the trip down, and the Captain told him we'd take good care of you." He held the wet umbrella away from Ma's skirt as he assisted her over the brass sea guard of the door to the companionway. "It isn't often we have the pleasure of ladies on board, ma'am." He helped Florence and Laura through. "No siree! It's mighty seldom we have the pleasure of ladies on board."

They followed him down the companionway to their cabins. "We hope you'll find the staterooms comfortable," he said. "Just call the steward for anything you want, ma'am."

"Thank you. I shall tell Mr. Monroe how kind you have been." Ma beamed at the purser.

"Just call for anything, anything at all," he urged as he left them.

Jaimy and Rod went back to the deck to explore the vessel. Loaded cabin boys left their bags and boxes and hurried away again. Ma closed the cabin door and sat down with a little sigh. She took Mc-

Duff out of his hamper and held him in her lap, stroking him absently. Laura perched on the edge of one of their boxes near Ma's knee, and Florence sat stiffly on the edge of the wide lower berth with her gloved hands clasped tightly in her lap. They could hear the loading noises and men's voices shouting outside. Inside, the cabin smelled of fresh paint and brass polish. Two lamps balanced in their brackets on either side of a mirror. Under the mirror a commode held the jug and basin, and towels hung from a rod on its side. A rectangular window with red-tasseled curtains admitted the gray light of the rainy day. Ma and the two girls sat formally, with their hats and gloves on, as though they were merely visiting and had no intention of staying.

Presently Laura, who was having her first doubts concerning the joys of traveling, said, "Aren't there going to be any more *families* on the boat?"

With a little catch of her breath, Ma smiled, as if she had just returned from a dream. "Don't you think it would be exciting to be the *first* family, dear?" She looked reassuringly at her little daughter. "You know, Pa is building a new world and we are going to help him. We'll be the first family, excepting the Indians, of course, to live in our own home on Prince of Wales Island."

In spite of the fact that Ma spoke in a tone that meant, "What could be more desirable?" Laura was not convinced.

"There won't be anybody to play with," she said, and her lower lip trembled as she looked down and unbuttoned and buttoned her glove.

Ma put her arm around Laura. "Don't be sad, darling," she said. "It's so easy to waste our tears when all we need is a little faith. When I first came to Victoria, years and years ago, I cried because I thought I was leaving so much that I loved behind. But Pa built our beautiful home and other people built houses, and soon it wasn't a wilderness at all. So you see, dear, all my tears were wasted."

"Let's get off this boat and go back to Victoria," Laura said, still not persuaded that all was well. "Pa can come home again."

Ma paused for a minute. Then she put McDuff in Laura's lap and got up, removing her gloves. "Pa helped to build Victoria," she said. "But two years ago he lost his fortune and—don't you see, dear—he went to Alaska to begin again. It takes strong men to build new worlds. We mustn't fail

Pa." She untied Laura's bonnet and put it on the upper bunk.

Florence could see that Ma was holding her eyes wide open to keep from blinking the tears out. Oh, Ma is brave, she thought. Bravest of all! The house we've left was *her* house; every room in it knew the touch of her hand and the rose over the door was a joy in her life.

She jumped up and pulled off her gloves. "I'll get the kettle out. We need a cup of tea," she said, removing her coat with businesslike briskness. "Laura, we're going to see Pa and the boys soon. They've built us a new house. We're going to be together again!"

Later, when Jaimy and Rod burst into the cabin, the kettle was singing cheerfully over the blue flame of its spirit lamp. McDuff, who had finished a cautious exploration of the cabin, lay across Ma's little feet as he had always done at home.

"There's a race—between us and a sloop!" Rod cried, his gray eyes shining with excitement. "I saw the sloop when we first came on board."

"Don't you want to come up and see us pull out?" Jaimy asked, trying not to look excited. "The wharf's packed with men watching the start. They're all talking about the young fellow in the sloop, who's bet his fortune that he can beat this steamer to Wrangell."

"They all say he'll lose," Rod said, "but it is sporting of him, isn't it?"

"They all say he's crazy and reckless," Jaimy told them, smoothing back his red hair and leaning nonchalantly against the door. "And every man jack of them is betting money that he'll lose. There are two of them on the sloop, but this chap who owns her is the one that's betting his fortune. They say he's sailed around the world. He's a deep-water man."

The boys were so full of excitement, they were having so much fun, that Florence's gloom slipped away without her knowing it. "I'd like to go and watch," she said.

"I wouldn't," Laura asserted, with a shake of her curls. "It's too rainy. I want to keep my clothes pretty for Pa."

"I see no reason why you shouldn't go," Ma said, looking fondly at Florence. "Jaimy will look out for you."

After Pa and the two older brothers had left Victoria, Jaimy had grown from a teasing, noisy boy into a responsible young man. For almost two years he had been the man of the family, and he made an effort now to control his boyish enthusiasm for the adventure of traveling. Because he was still growing, he had a young coltish look, even in his man's tweeds, and there was an energetic gaiety about him that he was never to lose. He said, "Hurry up, Flossie. Your escort is ready."

The deep-voiced steam whistle blew its warning as they went up the curving stairs, and by the time they reached the deck the dripping gangplank was being hauled on board. The fresh wind whipped at Florence's long skirts, and she could feel fine rain blow against her cheek. They moved to the side away from the wharf, but even there they could hear the shouts and laughter of the rough crowd.

Men were laughing at the chap on the sloop, but everybody was talking about him. As the young Monroes moved across the crowded deck, one passenger said: "I tell you, it can't be done. It's nothing but romantic foolishness to suppose that sails can beat the steamer. I don't care how good a sailor this—what's his name—is." Someone replied: "Beldon Craig's his name. And if you ask *me,* he's going to lose his fortune *and* his sloop in this venture. It's the wildest kind of nonsense to race through the channels between here and Wrangell. He's too big for his breeches, that's all."

Florence took Jaimy's arm and walked, erect and dignified, to the rain-splashed rail. With her other hand she held her skirts up at the back to keep them off the wet deck. There were no other women to be seen, and when the men became aware of her presence a hush fell over them and the loud conversation stopped. They made way to give her room at the rail. She stood with a brother on either side looking out over the rain-swept bay.

"There she is!" Rod cried, with a ring of pride in his voice as though the sloop were his. "I'm for the sloop."

The tall sail was rushing toward them, leaning strongly in the wind. As they watched, a figure came forward and they could see him working with the lines; then the jibsail flapped out and grew taut and wind-filled. The slim craft came tearing toward them until it seemed that the bowsprit would break against the side of the steamer in another minute. Florence watched, her face glowing with excitement, as the young man at the wheel, bright and shiny in his yellow oilskins, brought her around sharply. The boom swung over and the white canvas snapped out as the tall sail skimmed past, leaning so far over that the red paint of the sloop's bottom showed dark against the choppy water.

There was a sigh among the men on deck. "He certainly can handle her," one of them said. "He'll *need* to," his friend replied with a laugh.

Florence had tried to see the face of the man in the cockpit, but the shiny top of his sou'wester and his bright yellow oilskins were all she could make out. He'd stood, with his hands on the wheel, without looking up as the sloop raced past. Now he was coming around the second time, keeping a wide distance, and a cheer rose from the wharf. The steamer's whistle roared out three blasts, and they could feel the tremble of her decks as she picked up speed heading out of the bay. On the sloop a third sail ballooned out, and the water widened between them.

"He'll run clear enough now," a man behind Florence said. "But wait till he gets in the shelter of Vancouver Island. It'll be a different story then."

It seemed horrid to Florence that they all wanted him to lose. She heard someone else say smugly: "The wind won't last this time of year. He won't dare try the Narrows with the tide running unless he's got a whale of a lot of wind. We'll leave him behind at the Narrows, all right."

"Aren't they wretched!" Florence whispered to Rod.

"Even if the sloop loses," Rod said, "you can't help being for a chap that sails like that. Just look at her!"

The white sloop ran ahead of them, her sails spread slantwise across the water, like a sea bird on the wing. Impulsively, Florence fluttered her handkerchief over the rail. "Good luck!" she cried. "Oh, I hope you win!"

As a wave of amused smiles spread over the crowd on deck, Rod squeezed her arm. "Good for you, Sister," he said. "The Monroes are for the sloop."

The Captain made a courtesy call that evening and took Rod and Jaimy to the dining saloon with him. Ma and the girls had the meal brought to their cabin. Before they had finished eating, little Laura was yawning. "I feel as if I've been traveling ever and ever so long," she said.

Ma said, "We'll go to bed early and–just think –there'll be tonight and tomorrow night and then we'll see Pa!"

Even the boys were content to go to bed soon after their supper. As Jaimy pointed out, they would be at the Narrows early in the morning and he, for one, intended to be on deck to see the sloop go through. After the evening prayer was said, the boys kissed Ma and went to their own cabin.

Florence buttoned her nightgown at the neck and the frilled cuffs, and plaited her long, shining hair into a braid down her back. When Ma and Laura were tucked into the wide lower berth, she blew out the lamps and climbed into the upper bunk in the dark. She could hear Ma's voice, gay and gentle as she talked to Laura. Then there was silence, and she knew that her little sister had gone to sleep. She lay back on her pillow, conscious of the bed linen that felt different and smelled different than that at home. She put her arm over her eyes and smelled the fragrance of lavender delicately clinging to her sleeve. She closed her eyes but she didn't sleep; she began remembering.

She remembered all the years in the old house, and her own sweet room with its big bed and its south window facing the orchard. There were the summers in the orchard playing Indian with the boys and the winters with all the grates blazing and Pa teaching them to sing together like a choir. Then there was the little organ and her first music lessons; and the lovely curving stairway in the hall where Gregory played prince and princess with her when she was little, and the stairway was the castle. She thought of Ma's pretty sitting room upstairs, and of the dark oak dining room, and of the heavy silver and the thin china. She thought of Pa standing up to carve, and of Ah Lee shuff-shuffing in his black silk Chinese slippers, as he carried the serving dishes in and out.

Then she was remembering her girlhood dreams and all she had hoped her life would be. There was the time when she was Florence Nightingale in the pantomime at Bonnie Briar Seminary. Florence Nightingale was the greatest living Englishwoman, except the Queen, of course. Florence and her friends had been inspired by her story. They resolved that when they grew up they would carry the veil of mercy to the sick and wounded like this great lady. They had studied her "Notes on Nursing," and practiced earnestly on any members of their families who became ill or were injured. Her appeal to the women of England for more nurses had influenced them tremendously, and it was their dream to study nursing with her there.

Florence sighed, staring wide-eyed into the dark. And now I am grown-up, she thought sadly, and everything is gone—the big house on the hill, my friends and Ma's, all the things I hoped to do. The other girls will go to England and to Edinburgh, perhaps even to France. Pa didn't approve of going to France, but he would have let her go to Edinburgh had they stayed in Victoria. But what would he expect of her in Alaska? She turned over and wept silently into her pillow because she didn't want Ma to hear.

CHAPTER 2

When morning came, the steamer was plowing the water of Georgia Strait, running between the mountainous length of Vancouver Island and the rugged and deeply indented shores of the British Columbia mainland. Just ahead, Beldon Craig's sloop raced toward Cape Mudge and Discovery Passage, the channel that closed in dangerously at Seymour Narrows. At Cape Mudge the tide began to accelerate, flattening the wind-swept water and racing in swirls and glassy wrinkles toward the Narrows, where the cliffs of Maud Island

and a point of the mainland reached toward the rocky shore of Vancouver Island. The danger of the Narrows lay, not in the proximity of the gray cliffs on each side, but in the inexorable drive of the tides over a shelving rock submerged in its center, a rock that waited, like a monster, for its victims to be driven in and destroyed.

It was a rule of the steamship companies that vessels wait for slack tide before making the run through Seymour Narrows. All those on board the steamer who were familiar with the passage knew that if they reached the Narrows in the full rush of the tide, the Captain would pull into Menzies Bay, which made a safe anchorage at the entrance, and wait there for the tide to slack.

When morning broke, with the southeaster still driving rain into the gray water, many a passenger who had bet his money against the sloop cursed the unseasonable storm that gave such advantage to the sails. Many of them were on deck early, to see whether young Craig would dare the tide at the Narrows.

When Jaimy Monroe tapped softly on Florence's door, she was already half awake. In the excitement of anticipation she quite forgot the gloom that had beset her the night before, as one forgets an unhappy dream. She crawled to the end of her bunk, reached a bare foot down to the wooden edge of Ma's berth, and thus lowered herself noiselessly to the floor. She used both hands to open the door a crack so the latch wouldn't click too loudly. Jaimy and Rod were standing outside, coats and caps on, ready to go.

"We're going up," Jaimy whispered. "When you come, bring a biscuit or something, aye? We're starving."

She nodded her reply and closed the door. Ma and Laura slept on in the lower berth, but McDuff, lying at their feet, opened his big green eyes and watched her curiously. She dressed as fast as she could, pulling her stays on under the fullness of her nightgown. With impatient haste she buttoned the dozen little bone buttons of her corset cover and stepped into her embroidered and flounced petticoats. The bodice of her traveling dress had sixteen buttons, and she was careful to get them started right so she wouldn't have to do them all over again. She put a net over her back hair to keep it from blowing, and tied her bonnet securely under her chin.

Then she let herself quietly out of the cabin. The lounge, with its red carpet and wicker chairs, was deserted as she glanced around her and ran lightly up the stairs. At the door of the companionway she stepped over the sea guard and paused, breathless, in the sudden wind. The gray rain swept past in squalls and blew in under the boat deck, peppering Jaimy and Rod where they stood leaning over the rail, looking ahead. Still farther forward a small group of early watchers stood, all of them with hands thrust in pockets and heads pulled down in their turned-up collars.

On both sides the shore was close, rising into dark hills that were lost in the blowing mist. The clouds were low over the channel, letting go their stormy banners in a gray and windy world.

Florence shivered and stepped back over the sea guard. "Oh, Jaimy," she called from the shelter of the companionway.

The group of men turned at the sound of her voice and looked at her appraisingly, then resumed their watch with a somewhat divided attention. Both boys turned and came across the deck.

"At last!" Jaimy exclaimed. "It certainly took you long enough. The sloop's right ahead, and it looks like the steamer's got to anchor."

"We're going up on top," Rod said excitedly. "You can see a lot better from there."

"But I'll get my bonnet wet!" Florence objected. "It's even blowing in here."

"If you want to see the sloop, you'll have to take a chance with your bonnet," Jaimy said, starting for the steep, brass-bound steps leading to the boat deck.

"It'll dry again, won't it?" Rod asked, looking at her hopefully. "She's right ahead—the sloop, I mean. We've got to hurry if we're to see the whole show."

It took only a second to decide between the bonnet and watching the sloop. "All right, I'll go," Florence agreed. "But wait. Look what I brought." She held out three pieces of shortbread she had got out of Ma's tea box.

Jaimy brightened visibly. "Good girl!" he said, as they each took one. "Follow me and watch the steps. We can see best from right up by the pilot-house."

Florence held her skirts with one hand and gripped the rail with the other, as she hurried up the steep stairs after her brothers. "We're getting close to the Narrows now," Rod told her. "It's a fierce tide race, you know."

As they came below the pilothouse windows, Jaimy stopped. Ahead of them the sloop, with all sails set, was flying before the wind. They were approaching Race Point now, reeling in the tide, with the Narrows a scant two miles ahead. Jaimy's eyes were fastened on the sloop. "The danger's in jibing," he told Florence. "Just before you came up, the tide rips took charge and his old boom swung over with a frightful jar. He straightened out again, but if that happens at the Narrows, he's done for."

Florence looked at the dark water boiling and edging up, as it swept past the point. She hardly heard Rod when he said, "Stand close to the house, Sister. You won't get too awfully wet."

In spite of the weather, a few men had gathered in front of the pilothouse to watch. They turned as one when the Captain's voice suddenly boomed out of the window above their heads. "Miss Monroe, you'll get wet out there. Come in and watch from here."

Florence handed her piece of shortbread to Rod. "Oh, thank you," she said, not sure whether she had received an invitation or a command. Jaimy had told her that passengers were *never* allowed in the pilothouse. The young mate opened the forbidden door from the inside, and she walked up the three steps with her surprised brother whispering after her, "Lucky female!"

Inside the door she stopped, suddenly feeling strange and shy in this austere and unfamiliar place. It was a bare, half-circular room, containing only those things necessary to navigation. The quartermaster stood at the big wheel with his hands gripping the spokes, his eyes on the compass. There was a monastical purity about it, a feeling of discipline and dedication. Even the air was peculiarly its own, smelling of machine oil and brass polish, of charts and the sea.

The young mate closed the door behind Florence. "I–I don't want to be in the way," she said timidly.

Captain Jeffries was standing behind the quartermaster. "You'll be all right at that window," he said. "Mr. Jonson, give the stool to Miss Monroe."

The mate brought the high stool for her to sit on and immediately took his place at the window on the opposite side of the house. The window before her was open, and from her perch she could look down upon the heads of those standing on the deck. Jaimy and Rod were leaning against the house directly below her, so close she could have reached down and touched them had she dared.

The Captain paced back and forth behind the quartermaster, glancing at the sloop with every turn. No one spoke.

Awestruck and shy, Florence followed the example of silence, sitting straight-backed with her hands in her lap and her eyes on the sloop. She could see it clearly, sails tight in the wind as it raced along. It seemed like a tremendous amount of sail for so small a craft. In the cockpit the man in bright yellow oilskins and sou'wester stood at the wheel. He reminded her of a large oil painting she had once seen in which a tiny figure in a brilliant red coat was somehow the focal point in a huge scene. Now, in this seascape, with the white sails above him and the dark, whirling tide around him, Beldon Craig was just such a focal point.

As she watched, another figure emerged from the hatch and made his way forward. A moment later, one of the sails, one that was free from the mast, was let go and came billowing in to the deck. Then suddenly the sloop reeled in a tide surge and jibed. The gaff snapped over, twisting the sail, but the preventer, made fast well forward, held the straining boom and she straightened out again, running close in to Maud Island on the starboard side.

There was a tense movement among the watchers standing on the deck. They stared at the tide swirls that flattened the water and at the curling foam at their edges, boiling up as though driven by a churn beneath. The tide was accelerating in its outward rush, crowding the waters through a channel little over a quarter mile wide, creating a suction and a backwash of such force that it threw a geyser ten feet in the air over the rock hidden at its very center. Florence gazed, fascinated, at the gray rock walls and at the whirling, breaking water between them, where the tide raced through like a swift and terrible river.

The Captain's voice seemed suddenly loud when he gave his order to pull into Menzies Bay and then his order to stop. The quartermaster pulled a chain, and the distant clanging of bells could be heard far down in the engine room. Mr. Jonson left the pilothouse, and the Captain leaned on the window sill on the opposite side from where Florence watched. The quartermaster stood exactly as he was, staring at the sloop as though hypnotized. The ship's clock ticked off the seconds with metallic precision.

At the entrance to the Narrows, the ebbing tide set toward the hidden rock in a mass of unpredictable whirlpools which ripped apart in white foam around the rock, shooting upward in a fountain. Gripping the window sill with both her gloved hands, Florence watched the sloop through the thin, blowing rain, as it rode the savage tide like a gull in the wind.

Beldon Craig was hugging the shore of Maud Island so close that it seemed as though the trim white hull of the sloop must crash against the gray wall of the cliff. Then the sails shivered, the boom swung over, and the canvas snapped out full again. She swept away from the cliff, passed the monstrous rock in midchannel, and went flying through the Narrows, to vanish in a squall of rain.

The quartermaster let out his breath as though he had been holding it too long. Florence stared through the rain-gray Narrows and uttered a gasping little "Oh!" Rod sang out, "Bravo! Bravo!" and out on the deck the voices broke loose, each man expressing his views on just how it was done.

Jaimy looked up at Florence. "He was great, aye?" he cried, his eyes shining with excitement, raindrops dripping from his cap.

"Wasn't he . . . just!" she answered. And forgetting the sanctity of the pilothouse she turned to the Captain. "The Monroes are for the sloop," she said proudly.

"Oh, they are, are they?" he replied, his eyes twinkling.

Fearing he would think her disloyal to the steamer, she tried to explain. "We think he's awfully sporting—Mr. Craig, I mean," she said. "And besides, everyone's against him except us."

"Oh-ho! So it's Beldon Craig you're for, is it?" the Captain teased. "I suppose us old fellows have to take a back seat."

Flustered and wishing she could make an escape, Florence cried, "Oh, no! It's just because it's a sailboat—and all."

He gave her a sharp, old-seadog look and waggled his finger at her. "When you grow up," he warned, "you look out for the sailors. They're a bad lot. And that young idiot"—he pointed in the direction in which the sloop had gone—"will drown himself if he keeps on."

Florence felt her face flushing. She was already grown-up and Beldon Craig was not an idiot. Oh, why did she always have to blush! He was only teasing her anyway. She got down off the stool and started for the door, unable to think of a thing to say.

"Come now," Captain Jeffries soothed. "We'll get your brothers and go down and have a bite to eat. When I was a youngster, I was always hungry in the morning."

I'm not a youngster, Florence thought fiercely to herself, as he reached around her to open the door. She swooped up her skirts and descended the steps with dignity.

CHAPTER 3

The southeaster blew all that day and night, but in spite of it Florence enjoyed the run down the narrow strait when the steamer made the passage at slack tide. She was too shy to ask about the reckless young man in the sloop, but she knew he was brave; she wished she had seen his face. Then as they cleared the end of Vancouver Island and home was really left behind, she felt lonely and doubtful.

As they hit the rough water of Queen Charlotte Sound, the boat began to roll and Florence and

Ma took to their bunks. "We're quite all right, really," Ma told the steward, "but I think we're better lying down." He brought them toast and tea and saw to it that the boys and Laura, who was bright as a button, got special attention in the dining saloon.

"Oh, Ma, what is it going to be like when we get there?" Florence asked from the upper bunk.

"It's going to be all right," Ma said. "You know Pa is not a man to let misforune defeat him. It's true he made some business ventures that failed. He has always been one to try new things; he believes in progress. Where most men would have been defeated, he saw opportunity in this new country and now he is succeeding. He is a builder of new worlds."

Florence knew that Pa had come from Scotland to Ontario, and from there to British Columbia; and he had been successful until the catastrophe two years ago. Now his new business in Alaska was starting well. But Victoria was home. She had never known any other world. This new world seemed, so far, to be populated only with men. She couldn't get a picture in her mind of what it would be like, couldn't imagine calling it home.

"We'll miss home," Ma said gently, as if reading

her thoughts. "But we must have faith . . . and put our trust in the Good Shepherd."

Florence stared at the white ceiling close above her face and listened, as the boat rolled and Ma tried gallantly to encourage her.

"You know Pa wrote that our home is all ready for us at this place called Klinkwan; and the salmon saltery is already a prospering business at Nichols Bay. Of course it *is* too bad that the business is in one place and home in another. Pa liked Klinkwan as a home place, you know. And when the salmon season is over, the boys will come home and we'll all be together in the winter. We must count our blessings, dear."

Florence said, "Yes, Ma," trying hard to be gallant, too. The names of these unknown places seemed to trip easily off Ma's tongue as if they really had meaning. Pa had said Klinkwan was a village, an Indian village. She tried to imagine the new house that Pa had built there, but she couldn't make it seem real; she could see only the old house in Victoria.

Oh, there isn't any Klinkwan, she thought, and lay back on her pillow and closed her eyes. Then she could see a white sloop racing, but she couldn't make out the face of the young man at the wheel.

After supper the ship was still rolling but less unpleasantly, when the boys came in, red-faced from the wind and spattered with rain.

"We haven't caught sight of the sloop all day," Jaimy said. "At first it was so narrow and winding we couldn't see far ahead; then there were islands in the way, and now when there's plenty of open water there's so much mist and rain you can't see, and the sky's so cloudy it's practically dark already."

"I bet that little sloop's having a time of it in *this!*" Rod said, holding to the edge of Florence's bunk.

"This won't bother him," Jaimy said. "He's a deep-water man, and if the wind holds he's going to win. Why, he's sailed around the world, I heard them say so. They're all hoping the wind'll go down and we'll catch him after we cross the Sound. But *I* think he's going to make it."

"The Captain let me sit beside him at supper," Laura piped up. "And he told me all about Prince of Wales Island. He said we're going to pass right by Pa's place tomorrow morning, only the boat doesn't stop there." She looked very wise and bulging with information. "And then we'll get to Wrangell and there'll be Pa and Alec and Gregory to meet us. And Pa's got a boat of his own that'll stop wherever he likes."

They could hear the rush and slosh of the sea, as the boat rolled and heaved herself through it. Florence was far too doubtful to feel any excitement about tomorrow. If the Captain said they owned a fleet of boats, it wouldn't make any difference to her. It would still be the wilderness.

"Did you have a nice supper?" she heard Ma ask bravely.

The next day was bright and sunny, with a fresh breeze that lasted until they were almost to Wrangell. The air was full of the smell of the forest and the clean beach and the salt water. When the breeze died down, a long streamer of black smoke stretched like a scarf over the suds of the steamer's wake as she made her way among the islands. The Monroe family were in a buzz of excitement. As they were packing their traveling cases, Laura suddenly threw her arms around Ma's waist.

"I'll know Pa when I see him, won't I?" she asked anxiously.

"Of course you will," Ma reassured her. "He'll look just as he always looked." Ma's face had a glow of anticipation as she rustled around putting last things in the bags. She made McDuff's hamper ready and set it on the floor. "We'll get him packed last of all," she said, with her little bell-like laugh.

Florence had been out with the boys and stood now waiting, with her bonnet ribbons tied in a bow-knot under her left ear. With the sunshine and smooth water her spirits had soared, and now she was impatient to be on deck again. Soon she would see Pa and Alec and Greg—and perhaps the young man of the sloop.

"It's so lovely outside," she said. "Do let's hurry. It will be exciting to see the town when we first come upon it."

Ma already had her bonnet on. She helped Laura tie hers and then donned her mantle and gloves. Together they went up the stairs and out on the deck. Florence led them forward on the upper deck where they could see without obstruction, and there they stood, an intrepid little group in a world of men.

The air was quiet now, and the wild country through which they were passing was bright and clean-washed in the sun. Evergreen trees covered the hillsides, and above and beyond them the mountains rose, rocky and precipitous, capped with snow. Small beaches were close on either side, with streams running across them into the salt water. Wherever the streams were, the light green foliage of berry bushes shone bright and tender at the forest's edge. The water was so smooth and dark that little boiling circles and whirls of tide stood out as though etched on a mirror. Occasionally a breeze brushed lightly across the water, blotting out the clear reflection of the shore line. When it was gone, the reflection was there again, trembling, but so clear that even the eagle soaring over the evergreens seemed also to soar in the water. Gulls followed the steamer, coasting lazily on the air, and small flotillas of sea birds paddled this way and that among the islands.

Jaimy and Roderick soon joined them, fairly bursting with excitement. "Nobody's seen the sloop yet," Rod greeted them. "Of course she may be just around any one of these bends," he added.

"There's not a sign of him," Jaimy exulted. "He must be there by now. You know, I heard that sloop of his was built for racing."

"There isn't any wind," Florence said doubtfully. "Maybe something happened to him."

"Happened to him!" Jaimy looked at her, laughing. "Why, he skinned through these narrow passages before the wind dropped. That's what's happened to him."

"It wouldn't really matter if he won or lost; it's a brave thing to do anyway," Florence said, and Ma agreed.

"It's like something Greg would do," Rod said. "It's just like Greg." Gregory was Rod's favorite brother. He was slender and dark-haired and proud, with stormy gray eyes and a romantic grace of feature. Whenever Rod said anything was like Greg, it was the highest praise he could give.

"I'll bet he got every inch out of the wind," Jaimy went on. "I'll bet he coasted in to Wrangell on the very tail of a breeze!"

There was no laughing at Beldon Craig now as the men on deck stood silently watching. Everyone realized that he must have raced his sloop through every mile of the dangerous inland waterways while the wind lasted. They had been right in one thing, this was a man who knew how to sail.

When the steamer rounded the point and the old town of Wrangell lay before them, Laura hopped about Jaimy, clinging to his hand. "That's it, isn't it, Jaimy?" she cried.

On one side of the town old log barracks and

the blockhouse, relics of the early days, were white in the sun. On the other side the tall totems of the Indian village stood, dark and dignified, remembering the past. A few buildings were at the head of the tiny wharf, and a church and some houses spread up the hill beyond. Enormous Indian dugouts, some of them war canoes with totem symbols carved on their high prows, were hauled up on the beach in front of the village. Out in the bay a small, flat island bore old totems and the painted fences and houses of Indian graves. Between this island and the town a two-masted schooner with a black hull was moored to a buoy. And there beside her, with sails neatly furled, lay Beldon Craig's trim white sloop!

Jaimy was so jubilant he forgot to look for Pa. But as the steamer pulled into the wharf, Laura was squinting through the bright air, quite heedless of the danger of accumulating freckles on her nose. Suddenly one of her small gloved hands shot into the air.

"There he is!" she squealed. "I know him! Pa! Oh, Pa!"

Then Florence saw that Ma had already discovered him. She was standing, proudly smiling, but her eyes were wet. Her little handkerchief fluttered in response to a wave of his cap. He looked at her for a long time before he waved to the rest of them. The wharf was crowded with bewhiskered men and Indians, but Ian Monroe stood out among them all. He was six feet three and distinguished, with his neatly trimmed red beard. He was the only one there who did not look wild and bushy, Florence thought, save the man standing beside him. Then she recognized her brother. "Why, that's Alec!" she cried. "He's got a red beard like Pa's!"

"Alec, oh, Alec!" Laura shrilled, jumping with excitement as he answered her. Then she brought a laugh from all the passengers. "Ma, look!" she exclaimed. "Alec's gone and got whiskers, too."

Rod was watching the wharf intently. "I don't see Greg," he said. "Greg's not there."

Florence put her hand on his shoulder as she scanned the bewhiskered crowd, trying to find her handsome brother. She knew how much Roderick had counted on seeing Greg. "He surely would have come if he *could,*" she said reluctantly. "Perhaps he had to stay behind to watch the saltery." She patted Rod's shoulder comfortingly.

Then the hawser lines were darting through the air, and men on the wharf sprang to catch them.

Someone on the deck shouted, "Hey, down there! Anyone seen Beldon Craig?"

Florence's heart gave a sudden thud. Oh, it would be too awful if he were one of those whiskered men!

A roar of laughter answered the question, and someone shouted, "Sure we have. Have you?"

With a grim look Florence said, "Come on, Roddy. Let's get McDuff." If he were one of those bearded fellows, she simply didn't want to know it. She had expected him to look like Gregory. She didn't know why, but she had.

Rod followed her to the companionway. "Do you suppose Greg will have whiskers, too?" he asked.

"He'd better not have," she replied.

"I'll bet he has a mustache, though," Rod said.

When they returned to the deck with McDuff in the hamper, Pa was just coming up the gangplank. He had an outdoor look about him that made him even more distinguished than ever in his brown tweeds and boots. He took Ma's two little hands in his own and gazed at her lovingly. "Ah, my sweet Maggie," he said. "My dear wife. I thank the good Lord for bringing you safely to me."

Laura pulled at his coat and then Alec came up

and they all greeted each other, trying to be as dignified as possible because they were in a public place. Pa looked at each one of them, and they could see that he was proud of them.

Later Pa took them through the town to the preacher's house, where he told them of his plans. He told them about the Nichols Bay saltery down on the southernmost tip of the long island, and about Klinkwan farther on around the end of the island where their home was. "It's a wee bit o' Scotland, bluebells and all," he said.

Then he looked at Florence. "Flossie," he said, "ye've grown to be a fine young woman, and it's glad I am to see ye so."

Before she could recover from her surprise at this special attention, he went on to tell her that he expected her to go to the saltery at Nichols Bay with the boys, and to stay there to keep house for them.

"But, Pa!" she cried, looking at him in alarm, too shocked to think clearly. "How can I? I–I don't even know how to cook!"

"Hoot, woman," he said. "Ye'll learn soon enough."

Before she could do more than exchange a glance with Ma, Roderick said, "I can go to the saltery, too, can't I, Pa? I want to help Gregory."

"You're only a sprout of a lad," Pa said, pleased with Rod's enthusiasm. "But we'll find ye some light task to do. This is the big year; every hand will count. With a big pack this year, we'll be well established in the business."

Florence sat silent, overcome by this turn of events. Ma and Laura were to stay in Wrangell with the preacher and his wife until the furniture was brought to Klinkwan. Pa had arranged to have it brought directly there from Victoria on the freight boat. He wanted Ma to be comfortable until the house was ready; then he would come and take her home in his own boat. In the meantime he would take Florence and the boys to the saltery at Nichols Bay, because no time must be wasted in preparing for the fishing season. They were to leave that very night so they would be there in the morning and have daylight to enter the bay. In the Monroe family Pa's word had always been law. There was no doubt that he expected much of them and that he was confident they would not fail him.

Later, when Pa and the boys had gone to load supplies on the Monroe boat and Laura was in the kitchen helping their hostess with supper, Ma and Florence sat talking in the parlor of the parsonage.

"But—but, Ma!" Florence said, tears rolling down her cheeks at last. "I've never been away from you! How can I ever do it?"

Ma came and sat close to her. "It will be difficult at first, dear," she said. "But Alec and Gregory will help you. They've been housekeeping for themselves, you know, for almost two years. I'll speak to Alec about helping you. And it will only be for the summer; then we'll all be home together again."

Florence sat silent, wishing she could accept all this with Ma's courage.

"I'll miss you terribly," Ma said, holding her close. "But I'm sure it will all work out for the best. I know you will do it well and I shall be very proud of you."

The faint fragrance of attar of roses and the softness of Ma's silk bodice made Florence remember all the times that Ma had comforted her. But now she wasn't little any more; now she should be comforting Ma. She daubed at her eyes with her handkerchief. "Oh, I'm such a baby," she said. "But I can't even imagine being away from you!"

"You'll have so much to do the time will fly,"

Ma said. "And you'll look out for Roderick, won't you? He's still so young. And he takes cold so easily ever since he had pneumonia."

Florence smiled and kissed her cheek. "I'll try to be like you," she said. "And I'll look out for Rod. I do like to take care of people, you know. It's just the cooking that scares me." She felt her courage waning. "And being alone," she added.

"You must expect things to go wrong once in a while," Ma said wisely. "Things go wrong in the best-ordered houses. Remember to be calm and patient. When there are dark days, keep a strong heart and trust in the Good Shepherd to give you courage. And always remember, dear, that I love you. I think you're splendid."

Ma kissed her, and they both wiped their eyes because they heard the boys on the front porch.

Jaimy burst into the room. "You should see the Monroe boat!" he said. "It's a little steamboat." He held out his hands as though he were measuring a fish. "It's about this long," he laughed, "and it's called the *Sea Wolf!*" He sat down rocking with mirth.

Florence took this news stoically; she even smiled a little. If she had to become a sailor, she would. Nothing more would surprise her.

CHAPTER 4

When Florence looked at the *Sea Wolf,* she managed to keep her face calm and controlled; she was determined to live up to Pa's expectations. The *Sea Wolf* lay beside the slip that reached down steeply between the piling of the wharf. She was very small and somewhat the shape of a pumpkin seed. Alec had already got steam up, and smoke poured fiercely out of her tall thin stack. Her wheelhouse, galley, and engine room occupied most of her deck space and gave her a top-heavy look. Boxes of supplies and stacks of wood, chopped to fit her greedy firebox, were piled on the tiny deck. The boiler, which had two plugs in spots that had rusted through, hissed terrifyingly as soon as there was enough pressure to make decent headway. It would take fourteen hours, Pa said, to make the trip from Wrangell to Nichols Bay—a matter of a hundred and twenty-odd nautical miles. Because of the temperamental inconsistencies of the *Sea Wolf*, the Monroes usually came and went with the tide. Pa liked to make Cape Chacon before the tide started pouring out of Nichols Bay. To make it work out right, they were leaving Wrangell at eleven o'clock at night.

The steamer had gone, and the wharf was deserted and quiet when they walked down to the slip. The sky was pale, so that only a few stars could be seen, and the air had a strange neutral quality in which all color was lost. The bay was so still that as they stood on the wharf, silent and sleepy, they could hear the little liquid "plunk," as the diving ducks turned tail up and disappeared under the water. The pain of parting from Ma was dulled with sleepiness now, and Florence stood waiting to go on board and wondering vaguely how she was going to get down the cleats on the slip. She had packed Ma's little book of recipes in her portmanteau with the box that held her cherished nursing supplies. Pa went down first and spoke to Alec, and then Rod and Jaimy carried the bags down. Presently Alec came to the bottom of the slip and held out his hands.

"Come on, Flossie," he said. "Just walk down the cleats. Mind now, watch your skirts. I'll catch your hands when you get to the bottom." Alec was not as dashing as the other boys, but he had a quality of responsibility about him that gave her confidence. If he said a thing could be done, then it could be done and that was all there was to it. She took hold of her skirts and walked down, keeping her eyes on the cleats. He stood with one foot on the slip and one on the guard rail, and when she reached him he picked her up and set her on the deck as though she had been a sack of supplies. She stood midships on the narrow deck, feeling the salty draught blow over her from under the wharf and wishing that some time in her life she had learned how to swim.

Pa was already in the wheelhouse and Alec returned immediately to the engine room. The boys cast off the lines and the *Sea Wolf*, hissing and crackling with eagerness, took off into the tide. Jaimy stood beside her. "I wish we'd had time to go and have a look at the sloop," he said, gazing back at its trim white hull, pale in the strange light.

"*I* wish we'd had a chance to see Beldon Craig," Rod said.

"Wasn't he on the wharf or–anywhere?" Florence asked vaguely.

"He was asleep," Jaimy said. "He hadn't had a wink from the time he left Seattle till he got here."

Alec came out of the engine room and interrupted them. "Better get some sleep, Flossie," he said, "and you, too, Rod. You're both asleep on your feet. There's bunks in the galley."

The narrow bunks were built against the wall to the left of the door. Beyond them was a miniature cookstove with a dishpan and a frying pan hanging from nails behind it. On the wall, gray enamel plates were held in place in a rack, with cups hanging on hooks below them. Florence took off her bonnet and lay down on the hard lower bunk and Rod, yawning, climbed willingly into the upper one. Both fell asleep instantly and slept right through the five o'clock tea brew that Alec made in the morning.

When he came in again at seven and began rattling the stove lids in preparation for breakfast, Florence woke up. After a moment of wonder, she turned stiffly on the hard bunk and remembered where she was. She got up and walked across the galley, smoothing her hair and trying to shake the wrinkles out of her skirt. "I'll help you, Alec, if you'll tell me what to do," she offered uncertainly.

"You'll get your gown spattered," Alec said. "Here, tie this around it." He handed her a bleached sugar sack. "I'll peel the spuds and you fry them. You'll see 'tis nothing. Spuds and bacon and coffee, and plenty of it—that's the rule." He put a thick strip of bacon in the frying pan that covered the top of the little stove except for the corner where the coffeepot stood. "When that fries out, there'll be fat enough for your spuds." He gave her a long fork and a rag to hold the pan with, and then he went to work peeling potatoes so rapidly that by the time the bacon was fried out a basin full of potatoes was ready. "Just slice them into the grease," he directed, "and watch the splatter now." He handed her a huge butcher knife.

By the time three pans of potatoes had been fried, dumped into a basin, and stowed in the tiny oven to keep hot, Florence was flushed and perspiring. Her right hand trembled from the strain of wielding the big knife and her left thumb was stained brown. She had protested the third pan, but Alec merely said, "Tut, woman!" and progressed to the bacon. When he finished slicing it, she said, "Oh, Alec, how can we eat that much?"

"Just fry it up, Flossie," he answered. "And, mind you, don't cook the life out of it." With that he left her and went to feed more wood to the *Sea Wolf's* firebox.

Florence learned that on board the boat eating was a matter to be dispatched as quickly as possible, with a minimum of dishes and effort. No time was wasted with conversation or pleasantries. Alec ate first and then went to the wheelhouse; then Pa and Jaimy ate and lay down in the bunks to take a nap. Florence sat with Rod, ravenous in spite of herself, eating bacon and potatoes and trying to remember the big dining room at home, with its paneled walls and the silver on the table.

The morning had brought an overcast but no wind, and the *Sea Wolf* plowed along down Clarence Strait with Prince of Wales Island close by on her starboard side. It was a big island, about one hundred and twenty miles long, and deeply indented with bays and inlets. Its hills and mountains, heavily wooded with dark conifers, were shrouded with drifting fog. It stood between the Pacific Ocean and the mainland, and it was surrounded with tiny islands and rocks, like a hen with hundreds of chicks. Clarence Strait stretched along the inland side and opened out to Dixon Entrance at Cape Chacon, about three miles from the mouth of Nichols Bay. In bad weather, Alec said, the seas piled in from the ocean, rising into breakers off the cape and crashing into the islands that filled the mouth of the bay. On the south side Point Nunez extended into the sea, ending in islands and a dangerous reef offshore. The channel running into Nichols Bay lay between the islands and Point Nunez, and the tide ran through it like a river.

As the *Sea Wolf* passed Cape Chacon, the ground swells from Dixon Entrance were wide and flat, like slow undulations moving in under the smooth surface of the water. Florence, in bonnet, coat, and gloves, sat on a box in front of the wheelhouse, trying not to feel ill as the little boat reeled her way across the three miles of open water. Roderick stood beside her, feet apart, enjoying the slow motion. Pa took the wheel from Jaimy as they approached the channel into the bay. "Yon's the Bean Island," he said, indicating a wooded and hilly island off the port side. "Ye've got to hold off there to find the channel."

Jaimy leaned on the window sill above Florence, watching and listening to Pa's instructions. Pa had never been a seafaring man, and they were all much impressed by his knowledge of the sea and tides. He pointed out the rocks and tide rips and cautioned Jaimy about the dangers of attempting to get in or out of the bay in bad weather. Once they were in the shelter of Bean Island, the surface of the water was flat and swirling with tide. The *Sea Wolf* picked up speed with the inrunning tide, and the shore line, very close on either side, slid by in a panorama of scenic beauty. "Jiminy!" Rod said. "I'd like to explore these islands. Do they have names?"

"None that I ken," Pa said, keeping his eyes on the channel.

"Then they're my islands," Rod declared, "and I'm going to explore them!"

So the islands were named in passing, and the *Sea Wolf* turned sharply around the last one in order to clear a point that reached out halfway across the bay. Around the point the bay widened and stretched on for about two miles, where it narrowed into the mouth of a river. Wooded hills rose steeply on the north side and gradually into mountains to the south, where two streams ran down to a cove and joined at the beach. The water was smooth as a table top and deep green, and the hills, darker still, rose into the silent fog. The point behind them seemed to cut off their last communication with the world as the wild loneliness of the inner bay closed down and enveloped them. Florence shivered and looked about her nervously, feeling suddenly trapped.

When they passed the hills to the east of the cove, they saw the Monroe saltery. A narrow wharf stood out from the shore near the mouth of the stream, with the tide line showing darkly on the piling. There were two shed-like buildings at the head of the wharf, one of them dark and weathered, built of split boards; the other was not yet finished, and its milled lumber looked cheerily yellow against the dark forest behind it. Some distance to the left of the wharf, blue smoke rose straight up from the chimney of a small unpainted cabin. Pa pulled the whistle cord and the *Sea Wolf* let out a hoarse hoot and a great deal of steam.

Jaimy came out of the wheelhouse, looking eagerly about him. "It's a fine bay, isn't it?" he said. "And Pa says there's deer and ducks and partridge to shoot and trout fishing—and everything. It's a *place*, aye?"

"Y-yes," Florence said doubtfully. "But, Jaimy, just look at those little buildings! It's the Monroes against the wilderness."

Jaimy laughed and Florence joined him, cheered by his vitality. She had met the challenge, so far, and already the cookstove had lost some of its threat. Her courage returned. "We'll soon see Gregory," she said to Roderick.

"I see him now! He's just coming out on the wharf. See?" Rod took hold of her arm, growing suddenly shy now that he was actually about to face Gregory.

"Yes, I do see him," Florence said, getting to her feet. "Here, stand up on the box and wave to him. Wave your handkerchief and he'll be sure to see it."

Rod said, "No. Only girls wave handkerchiefs." But he did step up on the box and watch intently, waiting for Greg to make the first move.

As they drew near the wharf, Florence waved *her* handkerchief and called out, "Yoo-hoo, Gregory! It's Rod and me!"

Gregory stood leaning against the bollard at the corner of the wharf. Compared to the other Monroe men he was small, standing only five foot ten, and light of frame. He had unusual grace of posture and manner, but with it a stubborn independence that had often set him at odds with Pa. Both Gregory and Rod took after Ma's side of the family with their dark wavy hair, clear pale skin, and gray eyes.

"I don't believe it," Gregory called back. "When I saw you last, you were a couple of youngsters."

"Hey, Gregory," Rod cried, "I've just been waiting to see you!"

As the *Sea Wolf* pulled in to the piling, Jaimy stood ready with the line.

"Don't toss a line up here, Jaimy," Greg called. "Tide's too low yet. Just take a hitch around the piling. I'll take the stern line." He came swiftly down the ladder and sprang to the deck. "You do pretty well for a landlubber," he said with his crooked grin. He paused in passing to give Rod a friendly push. "Welcome to nowhere," he said, looking at Florence. "How did you get to be a young lady so soon?"

Gregory had not grown whiskers or even a mustache. He was still as proud and quick and scornful as ever, his eyes as stormy as the sea and as gray. Yet there was something different about him. Florence tried to tell herself that Pa and Alec were different, too. For instance, look at the way they ate fried potatoes in the galley; no silver or china—a far cry from the big oak dining room at home. But she knew that the change in Gregory was more subtle and deeper.

Jaimy had got his line fast at last. He turned to her, laughing. "Old seadog Monroe is the name," he said. "Do that well with your first muffins and you can join my club—the M.A.W."

"I guess!" she cried. "Monroes Against the Wilderness!" They both burst out laughing, and for the moment the loneliness of the green bay was forgotten. "I don't even know how I'm going to get up that ladder," she said.

Pa came out on deck to direct things. "You're a merry pair," he said, looking pleased with them. "Gregory," he called, "take Flossie ashore in the dinghy, will ye?"

Greg said, "Come on, princess. Where's your stuff?"

"There's only my portmanteau and hatbox," she told him. "Pa said I wouldn't need much."

"All you'll need clothes for here is to keep you warm," Greg said grimly. "There won't be a soul but ourselves to see you."

Rod helped to put her things in the dinghy and stood waiting as Gregory helped her in. He didn't ask if he might go with them, but they could see that he wanted to. Greg said: "Want a job, old fellow? If you'll ask Pa to point out the grub that's to go over to the house, and get it all stacked here on the stern, you can help me take it over on the next trip. It'll be easier than hauling it up on the wharf and lugging it over."

Rod said, "Oh, of course, Greg," and he was off with a new look of importance.

Florence sat in the stern facing Gregory, as they rowed toward the little house with the smoke curling out of the chimney. It was built of split boards, weathered to a silver gray, and she wondered how in the world they were all going to find room in it. Greg was watching her as he rowed. "It's a change from home," he said bitterly. "A horrible change."

Gregory, who had once been so gay and witty, had somewhere lost his gaiety. "Oh, Greg," she said, "I know you hated leaving home! But now that Ma's here—and everything—it's going to be all right, isn't it?"

Gregory's eyes darkened. "It's all right, I suppose, if you think it's all right to snatch a youngster like Rod out of school and bring him up to this

God-forsaken country, and to bring you and Ma and Laura up here to live among savages."

She looked at him for a moment, too shocked to speak. She could see that he hated it—hated the wilderness and the loneliness and the kind of life they led. It would be all right for her and for Jaimy, but it was not all right for Gregory.

"But, Greg," she said, "Ma will be proud of you, when she sees all that you've done. Ma says it takes a strong man to build a new world; and Pa won't neglect Rod. You wait. He'll have Rod off to school by winter."

As he looked at her earnest eyes below the little beribboned bonnet, Gregory's face softened. "I didn't mean to trouble you, Florence. Of course it will be all right." He ran the skiff in to the beach, got out, and pulled it up on the gravel. He reached out a hand to her. "Come on, Florence Nightingale," he said. "Bring the lighted lamp to the soldiers of the wilderness. The Lord knows we need you."

"Oh, Greg, you remember!" she said, and picking up her skirts she took his hand and stepped out on the shore of her new home.

As they walked up the beach, she looked at the little weather-beaten house. It had two long, narrow windows on the side facing the bay, and two small, square ones on either side of the door facing the wharf. On the forest side, a lean-to had recently been added. A chopping block and a pile of wood stood in front of it. The house was roofed with heavy shakes that made irregular eaves overhanging the windows. Water from a spring ran in a little stream past the woodpile, then spread out among the stones and sank out of sight before it reached the salt water. A clear trill of bird song poured out of the salmonberry bush growing behind the cabin, and Florence's heart filled with hope and good resolutions. I'll make it into a home, she told herself silently, that even Greg will like.

Gregory was pointing out the buildings to her. "That one over by the saltery with the stack of alder wood by it is the smokehouse. The larger one this way is the coopershop where we make the barrels and kegs. That's my job, and I sleep there, too. It's quite pleasant with its own stove and all."

"Do let Rod stay there with you. He adores you, Greg. He'd simply love it." She looked at him with glowing face.

He smiled, and this time there was no bitterness in the smile. "I'm glad you came, Sister," he said. "You've done me good already."

"You know, Greg, how I used to dream of being a nurse, when I was awfully young? Oh, I used to dream of going off to wars with Florence Nightingale and nursing soldiers, but this is going to be better. To be here with my family in a house you built all by . . ." The words died on her lips.

She turned, pale and wide-eyed, as three Indians, their coarse black hair tied back with strips of red cloth, stepped out of the forest near the spring. Two of them were carrying a dead deer, its feet tied around a pole and its long white throat stretched downward so that the head nearly touched the ground. In a flash she remembered all the horrors she had heard of about the Indian wars in the Northwest—how the settlers had been murdered and their cabins burned because the Indians hated them for taking the land. She stood, frozen in her tracks, clutching her hatbox.

"Don't look so scared," Gregory said gently. "They're bringing us a present. They'll expect something. Go in and make some tea. There's wood in the box and the fire's going."

In the next instant she was flying up the four low steps and into the house. She closed the door and stood leaning against its strong rough boards.

CHAPTER 5

She stood there, back to the door, with her heart hammering away in her breast and the strength drained from her knees. They were bringing a present; they would expect tea. Gradually the room came into focus, and she saw a big enamel teapot sitting on a shelf above the stove. Mechanically she removed her gloves and her bonnet.

The room was bare, save for the necessities of living: two homemade armchairs by the window; a table with benches on either side in the middle.

The stove and a wooden sink with a worktable beside it stood at the end next the lean-to. A galvanized pail full of water was on the worktable, and a big teakettle sang cheerfully on the range. On the opposite side of the room a partition ran the full length, and in this wall there were two doorways, both standing open. Florence took a quick peek into the one next to the lean-to, caught a glimpse of two bunks, a washstand, and men's clothes hanging from spikes on the wall. In a panic of haste she ran to the other door. This little room had one tall window facing the bay and a single bed, neatly made up with a blanket on top. In one corner a clean wooden box stood on end, evidently meant for a dressing table. There was no time to notice the feeling of bleakness the room gave her. She tossed her bonnet and gloves on the bed and hastened to the stove.

She drew up short as the door opened and there was Gregory with one of the Indians. He was quite an old Indian with lots of wrinkles in his face. He was holding his right hand in front of his chest, and she saw two inflamed and festering wounds on the back of it.

"Nurse needed, Florence Nightingale," Gregory said cheerfully. He gave her a sharp look and went on, speaking to the Indian. "This—my sister—good *tillicum.*"

The old man's eyes, like small black marbles peering out of the folds of his lids, had never left the girl's face. Now they traveled over every inch of her clothing and came to rest on her bright auburn hair.

Florence Nightingale was not afraid of the most dreadful wound or the most disgusting illness. Suddenly Florence thought of this in her effort to be calm. She began to roll up her sleeves.

"Put some hot water into a basin," she said to Gregory.

She picked up her portmanteau and lugged it into the bedroom. In another moment she was back, wearing a long white apron with a strip of handmade lace across the bottom. The Indian looked at the lace. He watched silently as she put her box on the table. It contained cotton and gauze, witch hazel, alcohol, salve, talcum powder, tweezers, scissors, and smelling salts. She put papers on the table where the old man could rest his arm. Then she sat down on the bench, bending her bright head over the old Indian's hand. He sat there as she washed and dressed his wounds, staring silently at her hair and smelling of fish oil and smoked salmon. He kept perfectly still as she worked. She worked so intently that she didn't even notice that Gregory had left the room.

She finished the bandaging and rose to put her basin and tweezers on the stove to boil, as Pa and the boys and the two other Indians came crowding into the room. Alec was carrying the dripping red liver of the deer, which he dropped into the sink. "This will be fine for tea," he announced, dashing water over it.

Jaimy began shouting about the cruel pangs of hunger he was suffering, and the two young Indians stood in the middle of the floor staring, silent and completely absorbed in the details of Florence's clothing. Gregory and Rod were lugging in supplies. Pa looked at the bare table. "Hoot, woman!" he said. "Have ye no got the tea made?"

She could only stare at him. Gregory explained why the tea was not ready, but Florence wanted to run, to vanish. She picked up her nursing kit, feeling alone and resentful in this room full of galumphing, heavy-booted males, and those Indians, staring and staring as though she were a freak. Here they all were, before she had even unpacked her things, standing around howling for tea. And Alec with that awful bloody liver. Oh, she wished Ma were there! They wouldn't dare to behave so if Ma were there. But even while she was thinking this, she knew that if Ma *were* there, she'd be serving the tea, quiet and dignified and pleasant.

Florence put her nursing kit away and made the tea in the big gray enamel pot and served it in gray enamel cups. Alec fried the liver, and Rod passed it around with thick slices of sourdough bread. Florence sat behind the big teapot, quiet and dignified and grim.

When the tea was finished, they all went out, every last one of them, leaving her in a welter of cups and saucers and plates. The Indians ended their staring and ignored her as completely as if she had not been there at all. When the door closed on the last one, she sat among the empty dishes and felt a wave of righteous indignation sweep over her. She got up and crammed wood into the stove, emptied the kettle into the dishpan, and put more water on to heat. She started in on the dishes with an angry energy.

Oh, just wait! She would write to Ma this very night! She'd tell her how dreadful it was to be the only girl in a crowd of thoughtless, lumbering men, men that plunked you down in a wilderness full of savages and didn't help you at all, men that just walked out and left you with all the work.

She snatched a big unhemmed flour sack off a nail back of the stove and commenced the drying. The stove had reached a red heat, and the kettle suddenly boiled over, sending drops of water sizzling and hopping across the lids. Florence moved the kettle back and struggled with the dampers, tears of rage pouring down her face. She wanted to cry, not quietly into a pillow but loudly like a baby. She wanted to bellow and bawl. The room had grown insufferably hot. She jerked the door open as though she'd pull it off its hinges and then stood there, looking out. The cool sweet air blew gently across her face like a caress.

The mist had cleared, and the sun shone on the steep hills across the bay. The green water, ruffled by the breeze, threw off bright glints of light. She could see Pa and Alec working on the new warehouse at the end of the wharf. In the coopershop, the boys were hammering and laughing, building bunks for Rod and Jaimy so they wouldn't have to sleep in the loft of the cabin. The Indians had gone back to the forest as silently and unobtrusively as they had come, leaving their gift of venison. Everyone was working, and only she was crying about it.

Suddenly she felt ashamed. Remembering Ma's words about being patient and having faith, she went in and tidied up the room. Then she smoothed her hair and got Ma's cooking recipes and sat down in one of the homemade armchairs by the window. She turned the pages of the little book to the one that read "Hints on How to Cook Meat."

Weary from the hours on the boat and her flustered efforts over the tea, she sat idly for a while with her hands relaxed on the book in her lap. Under the warmth of her hands the scent of attar of roses came faintly, like a memory, through the air. Outside, the bay was filling with the rising tide, its smooth surface pushing shoreward to cover the barnacles and seaweed and the blue mussels on the rocks. Somewhere a woodpecker tapped out irregular volleys of sound in his search for food. Florence's eyelids drooped, her bright head fell to one side, and she slept.

The rattle and clank of stove lids woke her, and there was Pa starting the fire. She jumped up, clutching the *Hints about Cooking*, and flushing with shame at having been caught so. In a moment Alec came in with a platter piled high with fresh meat. She put the unread book on her bed and joined the men at the stove. "I'll peel the potatoes," she said, looking about her helplessly.

Pa said, "Poor wee lassie, ye've had a lang day. We'll get the supper tonight."

It seemed strange to see Pa peeling potatoes while Alec rolled the meat in flour. It didn't seem right to see Pa cooking. As Florence unpacked her things, she hurried in order to get back to the stove. She didn't want Pa to cook.

There was a row of spikes along the partition of her room, and she hung her gowns as carefully as she could. Her light blue foulard, her green walking dress which was left over from her school wardrobe and would come in handy because the skirt was ankle length, and two morning dresses, one plaid and one brown, hanging from their spikes, were the only color in the room. She used the partition in the wooden box for a shelf, and folded and stacked her petticoats, her embroidered shifts, and her nightgowns. She put her shoes in the lower section of the box and her toilet accessories on top. She looked around the little bare room and sighed. She would write to Ma for curtain material and linen coverings.

Pa's gentle manner set her to work with renewed zeal. She popped the potatoes into a pot of boiling water and watched Alec carefully and methodically flour the last of the meat. He went into the lean-to and returned with a two-pound brick of butter still dripping with brine. "Do you think I could fry the meat?" she asked timidly.

"You're a good girl, Flossie," he said. "Put lots of butter in and don't let the pan get too hot nor the fire go down. Cook them—not too fast, mind you—until they're nice and brown. Then we'll make milk gravy." He put the butter on the table, a frying pan on the stove, and handed her a knife. Then he started peeling onions and peeled so many that her eyes stung and watered as she stood frying the meat, her expression anxious and concentrated. Pa sat in his chair by the window reading the Bible.

When the boys came in from the coopershop and gathered around the sink to wash, there was considerable confusion, but Florence stood calmly in the middle of it turning the cutlets. She resolved to make some changes, but, as Ma used to say, "Everything in its own time."

Gregory stood behind her drying his hands. "You did awfully well with old Eesch," he said. "He was proud of that bandage. He thinks you're a pretty good squaw."

"Gregory!" she protested. "How awful!"

"It isn't awful at all; it's a compliment. He means that you are not a good-for-nothing lazy female. A good squaw is respected in any village."

"I think you're perfectly shocking," she said. "But how did the old fellow—what's his name?—get hurt?"

"Eesch is his name. He shot a bear and thought he'd killed it, but it lasted long enough to take a swipe at him with a forepaw."

Jaimy shouted that he was starving, and Rod stood at her elbow peering into the pan. "Oh, do go away, all of you," she said, "unless you want to go to work."

With the sun gone behind the mountains, dusk had settled in the cabin and Pa got up and lit a lamp. Florence put the food and the warm plates on the table, while Alec poured tinned milk into the pan and stirred up the gravy. At the table Pa and Alec and Jaimy lined up on one side, and Florence and Rod and Gregory on the other. They all bowed their heads and Pa asked the Lord to bless the food and to keep them true in His service, to watch over Ma and Laura, and to keep them safe. "For this we thank Thee. Amen."

CHAPTER 6

Pa had invented a washing machine. It was made of a half barrel with a plunger in it, and it stood on a squat bench in the lean-to. It had a spiggot in the bottom through which the water could be drained into a tin funnel and thence to a sinkhole under the shed. To fill it, hot water had to be carried from the range to the shed. The plunger was a rather complicated rig which moved up and down and round and round as a result of someone's turning a crank at the side of the barrel.

It was customary for the Monroe men to bathe

every Saturday in the coopershop. At this time they would change into clean woolies and shirts and be all set for another week. Pa insisted that they change their socks and wash their feet in buckets thrice a week, in addition to the Saturday scrub. The soiled clothes were then washed in the washing machine.

Florence's first Monday at Nichols Bay was a day of sunlight and shadows, with big clouds sailing breezily overhead and the water in the bay moving in patches of ripples as though some giant were blowing on it. It was the first morning since she had been there when the day had started without mist or rain. She felt exhilarated and eager as she cooked breakfast, using one corner of the stove, since the great washboiler with its tin lid occupied the rest of it. Pa and Alec were to leave right after breakfast to go to the post office at Howkan, a village some forty miles distant. It was an easy run in good weather because, once around the point, the waterways were sheltered and deep. Alec had been out at five o'clock to get steam up, and after a hasty breakfast they departed, carrying the letters they had all written to Ma. Barring a breakdown or sudden storm, they expected to be back late in the evening. Florence stood in front of the house, hand raised in farewell, as the *Sea Wolf* reached the point and, leaning in the tide, vanished around it with a long asthmatic howl from her whistle. Her puff of white steam lingered like a cloud over the point and then disappeared.

When the sound of the whistle and its last echo had died away, Florence stood watching the cloud of steam fade into thin air. Around her were the many voices of the wilderness—the small bird's note, the sweep of the fish hawk's wing, the gurgle of the spring, and the indefinable movement of the forest. With Pa gone it seemed oddly lonely.

Gregory was coming across from the wharf, and Jaimy's hammer rang out, suddenly loud and real, from the roof of the warehouse.

"I'll help you with the water," Greg said.

The smell of the strong yellow soap filled the shed as Florence dropped the five sets of long drawers and undershirts into the steaming barrel. "What time should Pa be back?" she asked, when she heard Greg come in with more water to fill the boiler.

"If he gets back tonight, it won't be until late. He expects to see that lunatic, Beldon Craig, in Howkan. If he does, he'll be talking fisheries till all hours, or else he'll bring him back here." He clanked the pails down on the table. "The fellow's actually thinking of starting in business on this infernal island."

Florence was silent in the face of this bit of news. She took hold of the crank, tried to turn it, and found that it took both of her hands and all of her strength to make it work. Why hadn't Pa told her that he was bringing Mr. Craig? Perhaps he wasn't. Perhaps it was just Greg's way of looking at things.

Panting with her efforts on the crank, she called to Greg. "Did you . . . say that Pa's bringing this . . . this stranger here?"

"I said that Pa intended to talk to him in Howkan. He'll probably bring him out here to see this 'wee bit o' Scotland' if the man's crazy enough to come." He came into the shed and watched her for a moment. "I'll send Rod over to turn the crank," he said gently. "We want to finish that roof today or I'd do it myself."

His sensitive voice had been full of sarcasm, but as he went on it became sympathetic and natural again. When he was gone, Florence cranked with renewed vigor. If Mr. Craig did come, she wanted to have the house in order. She thought regretfully of thin china and silver and flounced curtains. He would think they were barbarians. She would put on her light blue foulard—it was very pretty with its lace collar—and she would gather some flowers and ferns for the table. Oh, this awful machine! It would be easier to do the heavies by hand or tramp on them with her feet! When Rod came in, the sweat was running across her white forehead. But she was going at it with a will to get through.

After two hours of steady work, the things were ready to wring. Gregory had changed the water for rinsing, and then he had strung a long line from the smokehouse to the coopershop and provided a pole to support it in the middle. He helped Rod to drag the galvanized tub, full of wet clothes, out to the line. Florence and Rod took the long drawers and shirts individually and wrung them out, one twisting at one end and one at the other. By the time the heavy clothes were flapping in the breeze, they had to arrange another line for the socks. At first they had laughed and made jokes about it, but now it was time to start dinner and Florence left Rod with the socks, too tired to do anything but sigh. Her hands felt perfectly awful, and she took time to rub sweet oil into them after she had hung up the boiler and put wood into the stove. She had cranked until her arms ached; she would wash her own clothes in the tub on another day. If Beldon Craig were coming, she must have something nice ready for them to sup on, even if they came in late, something dainty and civilized.

Deep in thought, she fried potatoes, heated pork and beans, and warmed up the venison stew. When the boys came in and crowded around the sink to wash, she gave voice to some of her thoughts.

"Don't you think it would be nice to have a sort of wash bench in the lean-to?" she asked. "It doesn't seem right to wash in the sink."

"What does it matter?" Gregory asked. "You can't make a home for a family of hermits. What's the use?"

"Hermits don't come in families," Jaimy laughed. "They're old fellows that live by themselves and think the rest of us are crazy."

The hot food was on the table and they took their places. In the Monroe family, when Pa was away, it was customary for the youngest child to ask the blessing. Rod said: "Dear Lord, bless this food and make us useful in Thy service. Amen." Then he raised his eyes and looked anxiously at Gregory. "And hermits don't talk or sing together like we do. I don't *think* they do," he added as they all sat down.

Gregory smiled at his young brother. "You're

right, old fellow," he said. "If I help you get started, do you think you could build a bench?"

That afternoon Roderick worked industriously in the lean-to, with occasional flying trips to the saltery to ask advice. Jaimy and Gregory finished the roof on the warehouse, Jaimy proving to be a mighty worker. He got on with everything, was light and bantering about everything, but he didn't share Gregory's cynicism about Pa's dream of empire. He didn't have Gregory's need for the stimulation of other people and the things of the mind.

The bright, sharp ring of hammers on nails played back and forth with the echoes on the bay all afternoon, while Florence dreamily and happily baked her first cake. She had changed to her light blue foulard and tied an embroidered linen apron around her slim waist. She had followed Ma's recipe with the utmost care, and now she tiptoed around, washing the bowls and spoons and the egg whip and putting them away. She paused with a broom straw in hand, afraid to open the oven door, and fearing not to in case the fire had got too hot. After half an hour she opened it a crack and peeked in. The layers in two flat pans had risen, but they were still pallid on top. She put one more stick in the stove. She warned Rod not to come into the room lest his step cause the cake to fall; she kept an eye on the door, fearing Jaimy might come bounding in. As she watched the clock, she dreamed of the room with a carpet on the floor, a few floral pieces on the walls, some lace doilies and full, flounced curtains at the windows; herself in light blue greeting Mr. Craig at the door, graciously, as Ma used to greet the guests at home.

When the time was up, she opened the oven door. The layers were shiny and light brown, and their fragrance filled the room like perfume. She stabbed them gently with the broom straw. It came out clean, as the recipe said it would if the cake was done. She sighed happily.

By the time supper was over, Florence was so flustered by the boys' teasing that she didn't dare suggest, even to Rod, that they go and look for wild flowers. "You may be a hermit," Jaimy said, "but you're certainly a lady hermit—queen of the washtub, as it were!"

"I see no reason why we should be any different than we were in Victoria," she said, trying not to let him see how annoyed she was.

"Woman," he said, imitating Pa, "ye'll no be having frivolous notions."

"You stop that, Jaimy Monroe," she answered, her temper getting the best of her. "That's no proper way for you to talk."

"Leave her alone," Gregory said impatiently. "It's bad enough for her to have to live this way. If she wants to dress up, why shouldn't she?"

"All right, all right," Jaimy said good-naturedly. "But I still don't see why we shouldn't eat the cake."

"Because I want Pa to see it whole," Florence said stubbornly. "Come on, Roddy. Let's go out and bring in the clothes."

The long days were at hand, and it was neither light nor dark when the *Sea Wolf* came steaming around the point. The bay lay dark green and still in the embrace of its hills, and the mountains rose to a pale sky not yet dark enough to show the stars, but with none of the blue and gold of day. The wind had subsided, and in the stillness of approaching night the blue smoke from the chimney rose skyward in a straight column. The moment they heard the whistle at the point, the boys went over to wait on the wharf.

Relieved to find herself alone for a moment, Florence lit an extra lamp and took it to her room. She smoothed her hair and fussed with her lace collar and refastened the silver and amethyst thistle pin that had belonged to Pa's mother. Then, glowing with excitement, she swished out into the living room and placed the lamp on a shelf. Oh, yes, Mr. Craig. We watched your sloop as we left Seattle, she would say as he bowed over her hand. Her shadow, with its slender top and full, panniered skirt, elongated and contracted grotesquely in the lamplight as she flew about, setting the gray enamel plates and cups and saucers on the table. Her cake, smooth now with white frosting, was elegant in the glow of the lamplight. The butcher knife lay beside it, peculiarly weapon-like in the circle of light.

Florence made the tea in the big gray pot and set it on the back of the stove to brew. She looked once more about the room, wishing that she had gathered some flowers. The cake stood, white and conspicuous as a bride, in the middle of the table. Elsewhere the dark wood of floors, walls, and ceiling swallowed up the light, save for the golden glow around each lamp. She heard the voices of the men outside and the door opened. For a moment, in the strange twilight of the night outside, Pa's figure dominated the others. He stepped inside, holding the door open.

"Come in, Captain Craig," he said. "Welcome to our wee house."

Florence stood with her back to the lamps, so that her small-waisted figure was silhouetted against the yellow light and her face was in shadow. The light fell full upon the man who stepped into the room, upon his wiry brown beard, his bushy eyebrows and, as he awkwardly removed his cap, the high bald dome of his head.

A startled little "Oh" escaped Florence's lips, but it was lost because Pa was introducing them and the boys were coming in. She heard Pa's voice ringing with pleasure as he introduced Captain Craig, and her dream was lost among the macabre shadows on the walls as the men found their places at the table. Oh, he had no right to look like that, to be whiskery and old and bashful, to sail the tall-masted sloop through the Narrows like a wild boy and make her think he was young, and . . . well . . . and . . .

"Jaimy can eat his cake at last, can't he, Sister?" Rod asked, laughing. Then to Pa, "Florence insisted on saving it whole for you because it's her first one."

Florence kept her eyes on the cups as she served the tea. For the first time since coming to Nichols

Bay she wondered if, perhaps, Gregory might not be right. What was there in this wilderness for civilized people, for *young* civilized people? The men were talking but she wasn't listening; her life stretched out before her, a long repetition of washing, scrubbing, cooking. And there was Gregory, so talented and handsome, spending his life making barrel staves in the coopershop. He'd never meet a pretty girl. Why, he'd never meet any girl! It was all right for Pa and old men like . . .

Pa's voice broke through her mounting resentment. "When your son, Beldon, *sees* the place, he'll understand what can be done. We need young people, Captain. There's a world of opportunity for the young lads."

A blush of embarrassment turned Florence's face pink. She was glad of the lamplight and the shadows. Of course this wasn't Beldon Craig. It was his father! She cast a hidden glance at him and occupied herself with the untouched piece of cake on her plate. Suddenly she was hungry, but as she ate she listened attentively to the talk.

"Aye," Captain Craig said to Pa, "Beldon is canny enough, but the young scamp with him is not for settling down. He tries to persuade Beldon to go down to California. My other boys will come if I send for them, but it's Beldon that's got the knack of doing things. It's him I want to plan with."

Florence got over her blushes, but her heart was tripping along at such a lively rate she could feel it pounding. She made an effort to hide her excitement as Pa told Captain Craig that on the morrow, when Beldon came, they would persuade him on the advantages to be had in developing this new country. With the Captain's schooner they could bring in their own supplies and take their own salmon pack out to market. The schooner lay in the bay at Wrangell, waiting, and the Captain hoped that his son would see the wisdom of remaining here to make his fortune.

"Won't you have another slice of cake?" Florence asked shyly. "And do let me fill your cup."

"It's a braw cake," said Pa, "and I think the Captain will agree."

The Captain did agree and so did the boys, and even Florence had a scrap more and ate it happily.

CHAPTER 7

On Tuesday morning the older boys were working on the water system in the saltery, while Pa went over the process with Captain Craig and talked plans with him. They expected Beldon Craig to bring his sloop into the bay that evening and take the Captain back to Wrangell. As Roderick helped Florence with the breakfast dishes, he talked continually about the prospects of seeing the famous sloop at close range. "Do you suppose he'll ask us to go on board her?" Rod asked. "He might not think of it, you know."

Florence said, "I think it would be quite all right if you asked him if you might. He'll have no way of knowing how much you want to go on board."

"I'll tell you what I'll do," Rod said. "I'll get some crabs this morning and we can cook them and save them until he comes. He'll probably ask how we got the crabs and then I'll have an excuse to start talking to him, and maybe then I can work around to asking him."

"Oh, Rod, you're a dear," Florence said, "and that's a splendid idea. I'll go with you to get the crabs, because I'd worry all the time you were out on the bay alone."

Outside, the air was full of misty rain and Rod put on his oilskins before going out. While he brought the skiff around and got the crab hooks, Florence changed into the old walking dress she had brought from home. It was shorter than her new things, and she had to hitch up her petticoats so they wouldn't show. She donned Gregory's oilskins and sou'wester and joined Rod on the beach in front of the house. They were full of lighthearted speculation and laughter as they rowed out to the point. "Of course I don't expect him to give me a *sail* in it," Rod said, "but it would be awfully jolly to go on board."

The misty rain had brightened Florence's cheeks and the yellow hat sat jauntily on the back of her head. "We'll have a nice feast of cracked crab with boiled dressing, and I'll make some muffins. That'll put him in good humor." Oh, it was fun to talk about Beldon Craig to Roderick and not have to be wary and fearful lest he tease her. She felt a great flood of love for her little brother, sitting there facing her with his legs braced as he pulled away at the oars. The click-clock of the oarlocks and the dip-splash of the blades rode along with their young voices through the silence of the bay.

Rod had hooked crabs a few days before and come home with three fine ones as a result of Gregory's showing him just how to do it. This was to be Florence's first experience at the sport, which required considerable skill and delicacy of maneuver. As they rounded the point, Roderick explained how the crabs came in over the sandy bottom on the far side. One had to thrust the long pole down quickly and stealthily and hook them around the legs or, better yet, the claws, with the big halibut hooks that were lashed on the end of the pole. Drawing them up was the most difficult part of it. It had to be done steadily and evenly, so that the pressure of the water would keep the crab from rising in order to free his legs. At the surface one flipped him quickly into the skiff.

Around the point they pulled in until they could drift in water about six feet deep. The beach here was covered with rocks and patches of sand left wet and corrugated by the movement of the ebbing tide. At the water's edge the rocks were scattered and weed-covered and the sand patches larger. Beneath them, the sand bank sloped smooth and shell-strewn into the deep water, with just here and there a rough knob of rock showing. The tide was almost at ebb, and they waited, poles in hand, with Rod in the bow, facing the islands in the entrance of the bay, and Florence in the stern, kneeling on the wide seat on the side toward the shore. Gregory had said that the crabs should come in at the turn of the tide.

They waited silently, peering down into the green depths of the water at the moving panorama of sea life below. Little sand dabs, no larger than Florence's hand, darted from spot to spot, looking so much like the bottom that they were visible only when on the move. Bullheads with wiggling tails nuzzled around the weed-covered heads of the rocks, and a sea urchin moved with minute jerks on his green spines. Near the surface a school of fry, like a corps of cadets, came into sight, darting left, then right. They paused to mark time with their tiny gills pumping; then left, right, left, and out of sight they darted with a few little stragglers bringing up the rear just a count or two late. A transparent jellyfish came pulsating dreamily from under the skiff. The silence was so deep that Florence could hear the small sound of the drizzling rain on her yellow oilskins. She was happy. Now he was really coming. She would find flowers on the way home, and she would make muffins, and wear her blue dress, and serve tea as Ma used to do.

"I see one!" Rod exclaimed suddenly in a hoarse whisper. "I can get him from this side. Keep watching!"

Florence looked up with a start. "Where?" she whispered, getting to her feet.

"Keep real still," Rod warned, "real . . . still." He had his pole down almost its full length and he gasped and grunted as he manipulated it in the deep water. "I've got him!" he said, drawing it up, hand over hand. With a quick flip that set the skiff to rocking he landed the big crab on the floor boards. "Isn't he a beauty? A big fellow, isn't he?" He had to work to disengage the hooks from around the frantically waving legs of his catch.

Florence sat down with a plop and pulled her feet up. "Oh, get him away, Rod," she cried. "He'll nip me!"

"Don't be scared," Rod soothed her. "As long as he's on his back he won't go far." Glowing with triumph, he turned back to watch for more.

With the end of her pole, Florence pushed the crab under the cross seat. He was easily twelve inches across and he kept reaching out with his great claws, opening and shutting the strong pincers. "There's one coming your way. He'll cross right under the stern of the skiff," Rod said. "Quiet now! Get your pole down. Don't hurry. Just sneak up on him and hook him under the legs near the front, if you can."

She crouched in the stern sheets with her pole about half its length in the water. The crab came gliding and running sidewise with surprising speed. When he got within reach, she made a jab but misjudged and came short of him. For a second he paused, claws raised and open, then he gave a kick and glided away out of reach before she could move her pole into position again. Before she could voice her disappointment, Rod had flipped another kicking victim into the boat. "Never mind," he said. "There'll be more as we drift along. Next time don't jab so hard; just reach down and hook him."

"It sounds simple enough," Florence admitted, "but the pole moves so awkwardly in the deep water."

She hooked her next one but not close enough to the body, and he kicked himself loose as she pulled him up. Rod missed one, and the skiff rocked with his efforts to recover it. "Be careful!" Florence warned. "We don't want a man overboard. The water's too cold."

"Oh, Sister, look!" Rod cried, unheeding. "There's a huge one coming, the biggest yet." He thrust his pole into the water, reaching far out. "I can't quite make it," he gasped. "He's going your way. Oh, do get him! He's a perfect whopper!"

Afraid to stand in the rocking skiff, Florence knelt and reached her pole down toward the monstrous crab. Startled by Rod's attack, he was running along the bottom toward the stern of the boat. He looked like a sure catch, not suspecting another fisherman ready to intercept his retreat. Using both hands to move the unwieldy pole, Florence planted it in front of him and dragged it back, hooking one of his great claws.

With a shriek of excitement she started dragging it in. She got to her feet to make the handling easier. "Steady now," Rod cautioned. "Keep the hook close in. Steady!"

The hook slid out toward the end of the claw as the big crab fought to pull away. She strained against the resistance of the water, leaning far out over the stern. Then she gave a quick thrust, hoping to move the hook closer to the body of her quarry. The next thing she knew the green water came up to meet her as she plunged into its cold surface, face first. It seemed to her there was a mighty crash, then blackness. Then she opened her eyes in the watery world and began thrashing about with her arms in terror. Her head cleared the surface and she choked and gasped, water streaming through her blinking eyes so that she could see nothing but a blur. Buoyed up by the air under her oilskins, she kicked her feet and flailed about with her arms, trying to cry out but succeeding only in coughing and gasping.

"Grab the pole, Sister!" Rod shouted. "Grab the *pole!*" She realized that he had been repeating it over and over, and that now he was crying as he pleaded with her. One hand struck the pole and she grabbed and clung to it for dear life. Shaking all over with the cold, she blinked away the salt drops and tried to speak to Rod. He was kneeling in the skiff, clinging to the other end of the pole with both hands. He was crying openly, his face distorted with fear. She could see him tremble as he pulled her in toward the gunwale.

The tide was running in now with its full force. It set in strongly at the main shore and the base of the point, which created an eddy so that they were being swept along parallel with the point. The shore line grew steeper toward the end of the point so that now, although they were not far out from the rocks, they were in very deep water. Florence was afraid to reach for the gunwale for fear of tipping the skiff too far over.

"Don't be scared, Roddy," she said, her teeth chattering with fright and cold. Looking up at him, trying to smile, to comfort him, she saw a tall white sail bearing down on the skiff.

"Ugh—look!" she gasped, shutting her eyes because of the salt water.

Rod looked over his shoulder. "Oh, Sister," he cried. "He's *here!*" His voice broke, and he raised one hand to wave frantically.

"Help!" he yelled. "Help!"

He turned quickly as the pole slipped in his

other hand. The water stole up around Florence's neck and chin and she screamed. She tried to kick, but her legs were hopelessly tangled in her petticoats. Her hands, blue with cold, seemed frozen to the pole. "Don't let go!" Rod pleaded, again holding sturdily to his end.

She was having difficulty getting her breath. She felt as though her stays had shrunk and were pressing her ribs closer and closer, so that there was no room for air in her lungs. There was a wave of darkness in which the metallic click of oarlocks sounded sharply.

"Hold steady there," a voice called. "Take it easy. Just hold on a minute."

The darkness passed and she could see again. A little white dinghy had pulled in beside her, and a young man with a blond mustache and the bluest eyes she had ever seen was looking anxiously down at her.

"Steady there," he said again, smiling. "We'll have you out in a minute." Kneeling in the bottom of the dinghy, he reached down and took a grip on her oilskin coat just at the shoulders. "I've got you now. Just drop the pole and take hold of the gunwale of the skiff."

His voice was quiet and soothing, as though he

were talking to a sick child, but she couldn't let go. She was aching with cold and water kept running from her hair into her eyes.

"Oh, Roddy," she sobbed.

The young man's voice took on a firmer quality. "Miss Monroe," he said, "let go of that pole and let me help you into the boat before you're exhausted." He pulled up on her oilskin coat and she felt her body grow lighter in the water.

"Give me your hands, Florence," Rod pleaded. "It's Beldon Craig. He won't let you go. He's strong!"

She heard a voice that must have been her own repeat the words, "Beldon Craig?"

She managed to let go with one hand and reach up to Rod. Then she gave him the other and he started pulling her over the stern, while Mr. Craig struggled from his position in the rocking dinghy. Finally she got a new grip on the gunwale. "Now hold on for just a second," the young man said. He let go of her coat and climbed quickly into the skiff, letting the dinghy go with the tide. Then, kneeling on the stern seat, he hauled her in with a firm grip around her waist. There she was, weak and sodden, with her streaming skirts wrapped tightly around her legs so that her stockings showed almost to her knees. She leaned forward, her lower lip shaking uncontrollably, tears streaming down her face, and tried to disentangle her skirt. Her hands were so white with cold that the faint blue veins showed in delicate V's on the backs. She made no resistance when Beldon Craig took them in his warm grip and began gently chafing them.

"It was a bad scare," he said. "I've been overboard myself. I know how you feel."

When Florence lay back in her pillows, sipping ginger tea, she shuddered but it was not with cold now. She was warm. Her feet rested on a sack of salt that Alec had heated in the oven. A knitted shawl was wrapped firmly over her flannel gown, and her wet hair was bound up in a big Turkish towel. She shut her eyes. Oh, dear, it was so awful, being hauled into the skiff like a sodden sack of meal. Every detail came back to taunt her—her hair sliding down, sitting in the galley of the sloop wrapped up in blankets like an Indian! Mr. Craig had been so thoughtful, sending Rod down to give her coffee and keeping that other young man out of the way. And then, when she stumbled getting out of the skiff, he'd picked her up and carried her—oh, she must have weighed a ton, soaking wet and all—and he'd carried her right into the house. Oh, it was so awful! The boys and Pa and Captain Craig had all come running and she had fled to her room, shaking like a palsied old woman.

She was glowing with warmth when she reached over and put her cup down on the floor. The damp spot where she had dropped her clothes was still there. I wish Ma were here, she thought. Ma would give him tea and he would see that we really have a home. His eyes were very, very blue. She raised her hands and looked at them as if seeing them for the first time. He was the first man who had ever held her hands. She groaned softly, letting them drop down on the blanket. They must have felt like something out of the sea, like little cold, wet sand dabs. She shut her eyes and began at the beginning again. Presently she slept.

She awoke ravenous and sat up, listening. The drizzle had changed into rain, and the whole house was alive with the tapping of its many fingers on roof and pane. Her door stood ajar and there was no movement in the outer room. She swung her legs out of bed and wiggled her feet into quilted slippers. Peeking out of the door, just to be sure no one was there, she ran past it to the window and stood, pulling the Turkish towel off her head as she looked out. The sloop was not there. The bay lay dark and wild, its water peppered with slanting rain. Small black waterfowl floated about like decoys, and along the beach the seagulls stood, all facing in the same direction as though waiting for something. She dressed quickly and went out to dry her hair by the stove.

A moment later Rod came in, lugging a pail in which were the crabs, boiled now to a bright red. "I'm glad you're up," he said. "We may as well eat the crabs even if he did have to leave. Do you feel all right?"

"I feel wonderful, Roddy, and half starved. I don't know what made me sleep so long. Oh, Rod, wasn't it awful! I was such a ninny to fall overboard!"

"It turned out all right," he said. "And we did get to ride on the sloop."

"I didn't even see it," she complained. "I felt like such a ninny." She brushed vigorously at her hair, so that he wouldn't see her face.

"It's a beauty of a sloop," Rod went on. "He made the other fellow hoist the sails and he steered around the point and took her flying right in to the front of the house. He's going to stay in Alaska."

He took the crabs one by one out of the pail and lined them up on the table.

Florence began braiding her hair. "Put the kettle over the flame. Just take the lid off, will you? We'll make tea. What makes you think he'll stay?" She went to her room and came back with a handful of hairpins.

"Oh, I just guess so," Rod said casually. "He talked business and locations and things with his father and Pa. And his partner said, 'Our hair's too fine for this country, Bel.' " Rod pulled down his chin and imitated the man's voice. "Then Mr. Craig said it suited *his* hair well enough," he went on, "so I just guessed he intends to stay."

Florence poured boiling water into the big tea-pot to warm it up.

"We'll have the crabs for supper," she said. "I'll make muffins for tea." She got the bowl down and started on the muffins.

"I'll be ashamed ever to see him again," she said. "I didn't think I could be so scared. Oh, I'm so ashamed."

"What for?" Rod asked. "I was scared, too, and so was he. He said so."

The door opened then and Pa came in, the raindrops standing all over his wool jacket and his red beard.

"So my lassie's up again!" he said. "I thought young Craig was o'er concerned. A dip in the bay'd not hurt anyone."

"Oh, Pa! Wasn't I a silly to fall in?"

"Tut!" Pa said. " 'Twas naething, as lang as you're oot again. But, mind ye, let the experience be the lesson the Lord meant it."

"Yes, Pa." Feeling the color rise to her face, Florence stooped and turned the muffin pan in the oven.

CHAPTER 8

During the two weeks before Pa and Alec left to meet the freight boat and the family furniture at Klinkwan, the Monroe saltery was a hive of activity. No one was idle. Pa installed a little stove in Florence's room, so that they wouldn't all have to get out of the house every time she sponge-bathed. With the stove, Florence's room became her private sanctuary: a haven in times of distress, a glowing and crackling comfort when her loneliness for Ma and Laura seemed more than she could bear. When the bread wouldn't rise or the pie crust came out like brown cardboard, after a morning of wrestling with the crank on the washing machine and preparing enormous amounts of food for the hungry men, she would think of the stove. At such times she would retire to her room and shut the door and sit in front of her crackling fire, rubbing sweet oil into her tired hands. Only the stove knew her tears, her prayers, and her strength.

The boys worked together on a seine boat to use in the bay when the salmon run started. It was like an enormous skiff with a wide stern platform where they could stand and pull in the gill net. Rod chopped alder wood for the smokehouse, and now he had it piled in two long stacks, each of them as high as he could reach. Enough barrels had been assembled to start the season, and Jaimy rolled them over to the saltery and lined them up for use. The day the *Sea Wolf* waddled out into the tide with Pa and Alec, everything was in readiness for the salmon.

The days that followed were bright and sunny. The boys explored the mouth of the big river at the head of the bay and came back with a string of trout. Florence picked salmonberries and they ate them with sugar and tinned cream. She found bluebells growing on the point and violets and bunchberry along the banks of the creek that ran past the saltery. On the third day Rod proposed that they row out and explore his islands.

"Oh, I'd like to do that," Florence said, looking at Gregory who, being the eldest at home, was considered the head of the house. "I think the outer bay is fascinating, with all those islands and narrow passages, and I do get a locked-in feeling sometimes. Let's take a picnic lunch and go clear out to the Bean Island."

"Suits me," Greg said, stretching and leaning back in Pa's chair. "I'll show you my famous cut-off to Klinkwan."

"Is it far to Klinkwan?" Florence asked. "Could we row to Klinkwan?"

"It's around twenty-odd miles if you take the cutoff and go inside the islands. There's a good seven miles of open water between Point Nunez and the islands off Point Marsh; it's more if you go out around Bean Island. If I were sure Ma had got there, we might do it."

"Let's take a look at it," Jaimy said. "I'd like to see the Greg Monroe cutoff."

Florence got eggs out of the case and boiled them while she made sandwiches and packed oatmeal cookies. When the lunch was ready, she put on her old walking dress and joined the boys, who had brought the skiff to the beach in front of the house.

She sat with the lunch beside her on the stern seat, and Rod took his place in the bow like a lookout. Greg and Jaimy leaned to the oars, rowing with strong rhythmic strokes that sent the skiff along at a good clip. In the outer bay they kept in the south channel, planning to circle the islands on the way back. The tide had turned to come in, and the boys rowed close to Point Nunez to take advantage of the eddies. In the bright sun the outer bay with its islands and narrow passages was enchantingly beautiful. The air was fragrant with the smell of the forest and the sea, and warm with the sun. As they approached the end of Point Nunez, the tide was streaming in through Greg's cutoff with such force that they could hardly row against it.

"We'll pull in here and eat," Greg suggested. "When the tide slacks a little, we can row through and take a look at the outside."

They pulled in to the shore among weed-covered rocks with the tide boiling up around them. Out in the channel the water was moving into the bay in flat, boiling swirls. It was pouring in through the main channel and racing through Greg's pass with all the power of the ocean behind it. Florence stood on the shore, gazing across the narrow channel at the islands, wondering how one bay could be so different in its parts. Suddenly a great silver fish left the water, flashing in the sun, and fell back with a splash. Then she saw another jump, and still another, with a sparkling shower of drops.

Rod shouted, "Look! A fish jumped. Look!"

"You'll see enough of those before you're through with Nichols Bay," Greg said. "Those are the salmon—the first of the run. Before the summer's over you'll be smelling of them."

"Oh, Gregory, how beautiful they are!" Florence cried. "Just look!"

A salmon rose in its sudden curve, only to descend again in a rainbow splash of drops. "There'll be thousands of them before the run is over," Greg said.

They all watched as the salmon ran up the channel, finning the water and jumping as they raced for the river at the head of the bay. "We catch our whole pack right here in the bay," Greg told them. "It's a horrible place to live, but I don't know any place around where we could pack salmon so cheaply. They'll just keep coming and coming from now until the run is over. This'll be our last holiday for many a week."

He had hardly finished when Rod let out an exclamation. "Why, look! Somebody's coming!" he cried, pointing toward Greg's cutoff. "It's a canoe."

An Indian dugout had shot through the narrow pass, riding the tide under the expert paddle of a native. In a moment it was skimming past them into the channel of the bay. "It's Pete and his wife, Kitty," Greg said. "They've come over to clean salmon. That's one thing we can be thankful for. It's funny how they seem to know exactly when the run begins." He raised his arm and called, "*Klahowya!*" The Indian replied, raising his paddle in the air.

"Where will they go?" Florence asked, wondering with alarm whether she would be expected to feed Indian boarders as well as her family of men.

"They'll build themselves a shack out of driftwood and a few boards on the other side of the crick from the saltery. They were here last year. They know what to do."

"The country's certainly getting crowded," Jaimy said, with mock worry. "We can't even row down our own bay without meeting people." He turned and looked out at the entrance through which they had come. "With a tide like that you can really make time."

"I suppose we should go straight back as soon as we eat," Greg said. "Pete'll need some nails and a plank or two."

"I hate to go back," Florence said. "It's so open and beautiful out here." She finished her boiled egg and tossed the shell halves into the tide, watching them whirl and spin until they filled with water and sank. At the edge of the woods she gathered bluebells and star flowers and wrapped them in moss to take home.

When they had all finished, the first rush of the tide was over and Greg thought they might be able to make it through the narrow pass to get a glimpse of the outside before going back. The entrance to the cutoff was studded with rocks, and the passage itself was less than forty yards across and only fifty yards long. It opened into a channel which widened into Dixon Entrance. The boys had to row with all their might against the tide, and as they pulled through the channel to get a view of the wide water outside Greg said: "On a day like this it would be easy to row to Klinkwan, but most of the time it's pretty rough out here, and sometimes it's so bad you'd swamp before you could clear this channel. Once you get around Point Marsh over there"—he pointed across a wide body of water—"you find shelter again, and from there on it's dozens of little islands right up to Klinkwan."

On this day the water outside was as smooth as a lake, and only the tide race in the Narrows reminded them of its power. On the way back they shot through Greg's cutoff with dizzy speed, and Rod shouted with delight while Florence nervously gripped the stern sheets. Then with the tide boosting them along they headed back to the saltery.

Pete and his wife had piled their bundles on the beach. Pete sat on a log smoking his pipe, while Kitty was dragging all the driftwood she could find to a flat spot at the edge of the forest. Gregory went directly to talk with them, walking the fallen log that spanned the creek. He gave them nails, shakes, and a few boards, all of which Kitty lugged across the log. By evening a shack of sorts stood on the flat spot—a shack that looked as though it had grown there and one couldn't remember how the place looked without it.

When Florence woke the next morning, the bay

was alive with salmon. A drizzling rain fell steadily and everywhere the silvery salmon leapt shining from the gray water and fell back in a splash of glassy drops. They leapt high, turning in the air to fall back heavily on their sides. Everywhere, their blue backs showed and the water swirled with their motion. The run was on, and even in Greg's voice there was a heightened tone of excitement.

Florence dressed quickly and flew to the stove, calling Rod to come and help with the breakfast. Afterward, she stood in the window and watched them pull out, first the new seine boat with the drag seine piled high in the stern and with Gregory and Jaimy at the oars, then Pete and Rod in the old skiff that had been used last year, Rod standing in the bow and the rowboat hoisted on the stern. She felt suddenly deserted. Then she saw the wood smoke rising from Pete and Kitty's shack and she was glad that Kitty was there.

When the tide rose high enough to make it possible to pitch the fish into the saltery, the boys brought back load after load in the old skiff and threw them up on the floor with long, curved prongs attached to stout handles. Kitty began working as soon as the first load was on the floor; later in the afternoon Pete joined her in cutting the fish.

Kitty stood at the cutting table, wearing an oilskin apron and wielding a monstrous knife with the strength of a man. She would grab a salmon by the tail and slash off its white belly with one cut of the knife, letting the rest of the fish go slithering through a hole in the floor to make food for gulls, crabs, and tomcod. The bellies were scraped and washed and tossed into their first brine. Later they were packed in salt in the kegs that Greg had made, the keg heads were put on, and the top hoop hammered in place. Jaimy and Rod did the packing and Greg put on the hoops.

This work went on furiously as the days passed, and Florence added an extra meal to her routine of cooking, a late supper when the boys came in silent and tired, sometimes as late as ten o'clock at night. From morning till bedtime she planned meals, prepared food, cooked, and washed dishes. She grew weary of the sight of food, the smell of fish on the boys' clothes, and the screaming of the hundreds of gulls as they fought over the fish that floated out from under the saltery with the ebbing tide. She tried not to show her weariness and disgust when Greg, reeking with the smell of salmon, came in night after night and remarked with deep satisfaction, "It's a big run, Flossie. A fine run."

After the salting was under way, Greg cut some of the fish for smoking. He showed Rod how to string the pieces with cord and hang them on the poles in the smokehouse. It became Rod's job to tend the fire, to keep a continuous volume of smoke with as little heat and flame as possible. He followed Gregory's instructions to the letter, and stuck to his task with such devotion that Florence couldn't even lure him out on the bay to fish for bass at the point. The day they took his first batch down to pack he rushed into the house where Florence was cutting the last of her dough into buns.

"Look, Sister!" he cried, holding two chunks up by their strings. "Greg says we can eat them for supper!"

It was almost two weeks now since Pa had gone, and Florence had fallen into the habit of dreaming away the hours while she worked. Sometimes she dreamed of meeting Ma and Laura with a big armful of bluebells, and sipping tea with them out of china cups; but more often she dreamed of being rescued from the cold water of the bay by the young man with blue eyes. In this dream her hair stayed smooth and neat in its net, and she wore her light blue gown, which trailed gracefully, though wet, as she was lifted out of the water without effort. It was a few seconds before she could respond with the proper enthusiasm to her young brother's accomplishment.

"What's the matter?" he asked. "You look sleepy."

"I'm afraid my mind was wool-gathering," she laughed. "Your fish looks wonderful. Put it here on the table."

Before Rod got to the door on his way out they heard the wheezy toot of the *Sea Wolf's* whistle and knew she had rounded the point. "I'll finish the buns," Florence said excitedly. "One pan's almost ready to go in. Tell Pa that tea is ready, and if he has a letter from Ma, do bring it over right away."

She waited until the *Sea Wolf* was about to dock before she put the pan of buns into the oven. Then she stood in the door where she could wave to Pa and Alec. But instead of Pa coming out of the pilothouse, it was Alec; and an Indian was helping him with the lines. Pa had stayed in Klinkwan. Florence didn't know just what she had expected with the return of the *Sea Wolf*. Perhaps without realizing it she had hoped that Ma would come; perhaps she had expected Pa to come across the beach with his long stride and say: "Into your cloak, Flossie. I'm taking ye back to Klinkwan to stay with Ma." In any case she was overwhelmed with disappointment. If Pa was staying in Klinkwan, it meant that he'd left the saltery for the boys to take care of and she would have to stay with them until the last barrel was shipped out.

Turning back to the room and hating its plainness, she could see the summer stretch away, dull and work-laden, before them. She would fill the huge ugly teapot over and over, and the boys would come in reeking with fish, even little Rod smelling like a kipper. She would cook huge meals and wash dishes and try to dry woolies on wet days, and so it would be all summer long. She clattered the cups down on the table, her cheeks burning with resentment.

She heard Rod shouting as he came across the beach. "Sister! Oh, Florence! Guess what they brought!" He bounded through the door. "And look! Letters from Ma! Yours is the fattest."

She didn't care what they had brought. She took the letter eagerly. "I'm going to read it, Rod, right now. When you go back, tell them that tea will be ready in a few minutes." With the letter in her hand she went to her room and closed the door.

Sitting on the edge of her bed on the side nearest the window, she opened the envelope. The faint fragrance of attar of roses came from the folded sheets of white paper as she began reading the small delicate script. The letter was so full of love and understanding and humor that she cried and laughed as she read, and when she finished she put it under her pillow to read again at bedtime. She was filled with fresh courage and inspiration when she went out to welcome Alec home.

At the door she saw Jaimy and Alec carrying a little organ—her own organ from home—into the room. Rod came after them with the bench. Her lips parted but no words came out. Alec said, "Hello, Flossie, how are you? They decided on this at the last minute. Ma thought you should have it. You should've seen the time we had getting it on board the boat. There's no wharf over there, you know. Where do you want it, Sis?"

"Oh, Alec!" Florence said softly.

"Here by the window's best, isn't it?" He smiled.

She walked to the little organ and ran her hand over its smooth polished wood. Then she sat down and pumped the pedals, running her fingers over the cool keys. Then she played a chord and a run and then the first bars of *The Sea Mews,* Ma's favorite song. "Oh, Alec, I'm so glad you brought it," she said, feeling that the world was right again and Ma was not so far away after all.

"How about that tea?" Jaimy reminded her. "I'm hungry for some of those luscious-smelling buns."

CHAPTER 9

It was August before Florence saw Beldon Craig again. And by August her life in Victoria, actually only a few months behind her, seemed years away. It seemed to belong to her childhood; she thought of it in terms of "being very young." By August she could row a boat almost as well as the boys. Gregory had taught her to shoot and, standing very straight and slim, she could clip the cones off the trees with the rifle so expertly that Jaimy looked upon her with a new respect. In the fight of "Monroes against the wilderness" she began to feel that she was really winning.

She was no longer appalled by the amount of food she had to prepare. She never thought of a pie any more; pies came in tens; loaves were always a dozen, and buns as many as she had pans for. When Pete's wife, Kitty, dropped her big knife and cut a gash in her foot, Florence cleaned the wound and sewed it up with a skin needle such as were used to sew deer hide. She cut up an old oilskin coat and made a cover for Kitty's foot and dressed it daily until it was well. In the evenings she played the organ and sometimes they all sang together. They sang a hymn before going to bed, because Alec, unlike Pa, was not very good at evening prayers.

But Florence had grown so shy of strangers in this little kingdom of her own, with just the boys and the Indians across the creek, that she looked out in a panic of confusion the day the freighter came in to take their first load of salmon. She knew that Captain Hunter was a friend of Pa's, but she stayed indoors all morning, hoping he would not come to the house. She was ashamed of the homemade furniture and the ugly dishes, and she was glad when Captain Hunter invited Alec on board the boat for dinner and only the boys came home.

It was all right when they were there just by themselves, but she didn't want strangers to see them living like that.

There were many days without rain now. The berries were ripe, and grouse drummed in the woods. She learned to cook ducks properly and to tell when the grouse and ptarmigan had hung long enough. She rowed up to the head of the bay and picked berries along the river banks, and once she had to run from a bear who was eating wild currants when she got there. She made blueberry pies and currant and strawberry jam, and she got so she could do it without the recipe. She filled the marmalade jars and the various glasses that had accumulated in the loft ever since Pa first came to the bay.

One day, when she was filling the last of a dozen jars with wild strawberry jam and the house was full of the strawberry fragrance, there came a knock at the door. She thought right away it was one of the Indians. Who else would knock? "Come in," she called, scraping the last pink juice from the kettle. She heard the door open and turned, smiling, the big kettle in one hand and the dripping spoon in the other.

Beldon Craig stood in the door holding half a dozen large mallard ducks by their red feet.

Florence said, "Oh," her smile fading into a startled gasp.

He was bare-headed and smiling and he bowed to her. "How do you do, Miss Monroe?" he said. "I do come at the most awkward times, don't I?"

"I—I thought it was Indians," she said, feeling her heart pounding in her throat. His blue eyes were laughing, but he stood there waiting politely. What a crazy thing to say, she thought, feeling her cheeks flush. "Please come in, Mr. Craig," she said. "I'm sorry everything's in such a—in such a *stew*." A big pink drop plopped from the end of the spoon as she turned to put the kettle in the sink.

"I've brought you some ducks," he said, "and I told your brother Jaimy that he was to pick them or I wouldn't give them to you. Father wanted to go to Klinkwan and we stopped in to ask you to sail around with us."

"To Klinkwan? To see Ma?" She looked at him unbelievingly. "Oh, I wish we could go," she said. "But there's so much to do—Alec says we can't go until the season's over." She looked wistfully out at the sunshine. It was a beautiful morning.

"Tell me where to put the ducks," he said, "and

I'll give you a hand straightening up. Your brother Alexander said that you and Roderick may go with us. I've already asked him. We must get you back tonight. If you consent to go, we should start as soon as we can." He walked across the room to the lean-to. "Shall I put the ducks in here?" he asked.

"Oh, I'd love to go," she said. "Oh, thank you!" She looked around at the confusion of jam and utensils. Beldon Craig still held the ducks. "Yes, do put them in the lean-to. The boys always hang the ducks there." Oh, how awful this is, she thought. Aloud she said, "I'm so sorry everything's in such a . . ."

"In such a stew?" he finished for her, and they both burst into laughter. "Please let me help you, Miss Monroe."

At that moment Rod came bounding through the door. "We're going to Klinkwan in the sloop!" he cried excitedly. He looked at Florence and started to laugh. "You've got jam on your nose, Sister."

Beldon Craig said, "Look here, young man! You and I are going to wash up these things while your sister gets ready. You want to go on that sail, don't you?"

"Yes, *sir!*" Rod said. "Where'll we begin? Do hurry, Florence."

Her color rose and faded and rose again as she filled a basin with warm water and flew to her room. Oh, how nice he is, she thought, how courteous and kind; and he's like Gregory. Only he's fair instead of dark, and merry instead of stormy; but he's attractive, like Greg. She hastily bathed her face and hands and put on the plaid skirt and the many-buttoned bodice of her new traveling dress. She was shaking with excitement and trying to be calm. He would see Ma and their house in Klinkwan, and then he would know they were not barbarians. She put on her bonnet and tied its ribbons under her ear, took a final peek into the small mirror, and started for the door. Gloves! She dashed back and took her blue gloves from their box. Then, with her little velvet reticule hanging from her wrist, she walked into the outer room, smoothing her gloves on as she went.

The pans and spoons were put away; the glasses and jars of strawberry jam were lined up in neat rows at one end of the table. Rod was gone. Young Mr. Craig bowed and offered her his arm. She had never taken a young man's arm, except Greg's, in play. She found herself gripped in shyness so acute, so panicky, that she could only stand fumbling with the button on her glove. Oh, why had Rod left? She looked down at her glove, hoping he wouldn't see that she was blushing.

When he spoke, his voice was so natural and friendly that her heart quieted and she could look at him again. "Shall we take some of this luscious jam to your mother?" he asked.

"Oh, yes!" she said, finding her voice again. "I do want to take something to Ma. There are some jars in the lean-to with papers on; these are still too hot." He went immediately to get them, while she found a basket to put them in. When he returned to the room, she had lifted a bunch of bluebells from their pitcher and stood holding them by their dripping stems. "Ma loves bluebells," she said. "Do you think these will keep if we take them in a can of water?"

Then Rod was at the door again calling her to hurry, and they all went out on the beach together, with Beldon Craig carrying the jam. With a firm grip on her skirts, Florence walked carefully over the stones to where Captain Craig and Alec were standing near the sloop's dinghy. Jaimy and Greg were on the ramp that led down from the back of the saltery. They had been packing salmon, and their long oilskin aprons were shiny and wet. Gregory turned with a wave of his hand and came toward them. Florence raised her hand and called, "Oh, Jaimy!" But he turned away as though he hadn't heard and went into the building. He wants to come, she thought; oh, he wants to come awfully.

Captain Craig was telling Alec that he would have them back before dark, and Florence felt, for the first time, how much the boys depended upon her, how closely they were all bound together in this hill-surrounded bay. "Alec," she said anxiously, "you're sure you can manage all right, about dinner and supper and everything?"

Alec, matter of fact as usual, said seriously, "We can make out all right for today."

The dinghy looked awfully small, and when they all got in and pushed off, with Beldon Craig in the bow, the Captain rowing, and herself and Rod squeezed into the stern seat, the water was right up to the gunwales. They had to sit very still as they rowed out to the sloop.

From the beach Gregory called, "Tell Ma I'll be around the point to see her as soon as the season lets up."

"I will," she answered, not daring to turn for fear of tipping the dinghy.

The white sloop rode at anchor, and she kept

her eyes on its tall mast and remembered how it had swept, sails tight in the wind, in the race through the Narrows. When she got out of the dinghy, she did her best to look calm and brave, as Captain Craig and his son took her elbows and lifted her on board. She tried not to remember how awful, how perfectly dreadful, her first boarding had been. It was so difficult, with long skirts, to be dignified and graceful getting in and out of boats. In the cockpit she sat stiffly on the hard seat, trying to seem composed and to think of something appropriate to talk about. The men were busy with the lines and the sail, and Rod was helping with the anchor.

She looked back at the saltery and waved her handkerchief at Greg and Alec, who had come out on the wharf. But Jaimy was not to be seen. She could imagine him in there working—a layer of salmon, a layer of salt—pretending he didn't care. And all the time he cared so much that he couldn't even behave right. She wished that Alec were not quite so conscientious about the work. Jaimy would have loved a ride in the sloop.

The big sail hung in the still air, and Beldon Craig came aft and jumped into the cockpit. "Wish for a breeze," he said, standing at the wheel and looking at her. "We only need a little one. There's enough wind outside."

How blue his eyes are, she thought, as the sloop wheeled languidly in the tide. "There'll be a breeze," she said, looking skyward where white clouds drifted far above the wooded hills. "There's one near the point."

They could see the little breezes travel across the bay, stirring its surface; then from the river a light puff of wind ruffled the water as it blew toward them. The sail flapped as though shaking itself out of sleep, and the trim ship leaned slightly as it filled, and glided out past the point and into the narrow channel of the outer bay. As they passed the islands and headed out around Bean Island, Florence pointed out Greg's cutoff. Rod came back and told of the tide and their day in the skiff. Exhilarated and happy, Florence forgot her shyness in the excitement and pleasure of sailing. As they came around the island, the sloop picked up a flying speed in the fresh wind. The water rushed past as she dipped and rose lightly in the swell from the open sea. They could look out across Dixon Entrance to the hazy horizon, while on their starboard side the wooded hills and mountains of the island rose darkly from a sparkling sea.

At first Florence gripped the rail, excited but a little fearful, as the sea swept past so close to her hand. Then she grew accustomed to it and settled back, feeling safe and happy. The wind blew color into her cheeks and the sun brought little freckles out across her nose. She gave an exclamation of delight as they entered the passage among the innumerable little islands of Cordova Bay. The water here was blue instead of green, and sea birds were everywhere.

"I thought you would like this side of the island, Miss Monroe," Belden Craig said. "Your father has chosen a beautiful spot for your home."

"What a place to explore!" Rod cried. "Let's get a dugout and paddle around when we come here to live."

"You'll have to watch the tide," Mr. Craig cautioned him. "We're building at Thorn Bay," he went on. "It isn't as pretty as this, but it's more accessible."

Florence stole a glance at him, thinking how well the blond mustache became him. His chin was firm, and his teeth fine and white when he smiled. He wore a skipper's cap at a debonair angle, and when he turned and looked at her, catching her unawares, she blushed and looked away. "It's really lovely here," she said, feeling that some remark was necessary.

"Really lovely," he agreed, looking at her again.

Captain Craig, who had gone below after the sloop rounded the point, now stuck his head up through the hatchway, his bushy face smiling. "Anybody hungry?" he asked.

"Yes, sir," Rod said promptly.

"Let's have the ducks out here," young Mr. Craig suggested. "It would be too bad for Miss Monroe to miss any of this scenery. We'll soon be turning in to Klinkwan."

"May I help?" Florence asked politely.

"Oh, let me." Rod jumped up and followed the retreating figure of the captain.

They ate cold roast duck and bread and butter in the cockpit, Captain Craig and his son taking turns at the wheel. Beldon Craig sat beside Florence and showed her how to pull the duck apart so that it could be eaten in the hands without too much awkwardness. He put her gloves in his pocket so they wouldn't blow away. When they had finished, he brought a basin and towel from the galley so that she could wash her hands. Then he returned the gloves, holding them for a moment before he gave them to her. Florence, flustered and shy again, turned her eyes away from his gaze.

When the sloop glided into the cove where the old village of Klinkwan stood, with its many totems and its haze of blue smoke, Florence was beside herself with joy. With a little cry she stood up and looked shoreward. There . . . there was home! The big house stood some distance from the village, smoke curling lazily up from its chimney. It seemed enormous with its two stories and its clean white paint. In front of it the beach ran up and leveled off in grass and flowers, and there stood the house, the wild grass for its garden and, behind it, the forest for its park. The hills rolled away gently, and the whole country around was bright and picturesquely beautiful.

As she watched, the door of the house opened and Laura came and stood on the porch, watching the sloop. "Oh, Laura!" Florence called, waving her handkerchief. Laura ran forward, then dashed back into the house, and in a moment Ma was there.

"Oh, Roddy," Florence cried. "There she is! There's Ma!"

Suddenly tears filled her eyes and she couldn't see for the blur. Oh, dear! she thought, and dabbed her eyes with her handkerchief. The men were busy lowering sail, dropping the anchor, and bringing up the dinghy. Pa came striding along the beach from another low building nearer to the village. He stood waiting as they rowed ashore.

"We've come for a visit, Pa," Florence said, giving him a flustered little hug. "Alec said we might come for the day. The Craigs were so kind to bring us!" With a quick glance at all of them, she turned and, picking up her skirts, ran as fast as she could go to the house. Laura met her and hung on her waist as she went up the path to the door.

Then she was in Ma's arms, and they were hugging each other and scattering tears and laughing. "Oh, you do smell so good," Florence said. "Oh, I have missed you so!"

Then she remembered the bluebells and jam.

Rod dashed up to kiss Ma and stuttered in his attempts to tell her everything at once, and the men came to pay their respects before going to see Pa's store. The jam and the bluebells were brought from the dinghy by Beldon Craig, who gave them to Florence with laughing eyes. Then, when the men had gone and Laura took Rod to show him her special haunts, Florence presented her gifts to Ma. Ma said, "Oh, Florence, you have done so well. I'm so proud of you!"

As they turned to go into the house, Florence saw the rose bush by the door. A bit of the wild soil there had been turned and cultivated. From it grew a rose bush, reaching one young branch out to the wall of the house. Its foliage was thick and green. She looked at it, remembering the pink climber in Victoria. A rose bush for Ma—a rose in the wilderness!

"Pa sent for it, even before the house was finished, and planted it here for me," Ma said, watching her. "It will bloom next year, I'm certain."

"And it will climb up to your window, just like the one at home," Florence said, hugging her again.

"We'll put on the kettle," Ma said, "and then you must see the house."

Everything was there—the carpets, the rocking chairs, the big dining room furniture. The old clock stood in the hall. The kitchen was large, with windows looking over the wild grass to the bushes and trees beyond. And McDuff was there, sleeping under the stove as though he had never lived anywhere else. Upstairs, the bedrooms were furnished and waiting for the family. "Oh, Ma," Florence said, putting her bonnet and gloves on the bed in Ma's fragrant room, "we'll have a lovely winter. We'll bring the organ back and we'll make puddings for Christmas!"

Glowing with plans, they went downstairs to lay out the thin china and the silver for tea. Florence told Ma about the boys and the saltery. They laughed over her struggles with the washing machine; everything seemed amusing in the telling. When Pa came in with their guests, they hadn't half finished.

"Ye sound like a pair of o' magpies with all this woman talk," he said, but they could see that he was pleased.

They sat in the dining room, and Ma poured tea from the big silver teapot and Florence passed sugar buns and shortbread on Dresden cake plates. With delicate questions Ma drew talk from Captain Craig. He was taking his schooner to the States in the fall, and Pa was welcome to go with him to make purchases for the following season. The schooner could carry freight for both of them. They talked of plans, of developments, of the future.

Florence sipped her tea happily. Oh, she was proud of Ma! She looked at the lace doilies on the cherry-wood table and at Pa's stuffed pheasant standing proudly on the sideboard. She glanced at

Beldon Craig's handsome young face. When she made a move to rise in order to pass the buns again, he sprang to his feet. "Permit me," he said gallantly, and passed them for her. She could see that Ma liked Beldon Craig.

CHAPTER 10

By the end of August the last keg of salmon had been filled; the nights were dark again; and every evening the little bears came down to glean the last berries from the bushes at the head of the bay. Pete and Kitty and the other Indian tied up their belongings in a blanket and went away one morning, stirring the smooth green water into whirls with their unerring paddles. In the warehouse the hooped barrels stood in fat rows, awaiting the arrival of the freight boat. The sound of saw and plane came from the coopershop, where the boys made barrel staves for next year's catch.

For Florence the days glided by in a dream, not a definite dream, but a general dream of happiness which offered no questions and needed no answers. She didn't know when she would see Beldon Craig again, but she knew she would see him. Mostly she was happy because Ma knew him now. The Monroes and the Craigs were friends. And she knew, even with the miles of sea between them, that he would come. But this knowledge was her secret, too delicate for any ears, except Ma's when she should see her again.

The freight boat was due in by the middle of September at the latest, and perhaps before. The last of the pack would be shipped, and then they would board up the place for the winter and get on the *Sea Wolf* and steam around the island to Klinkwan. They would go home. Pa's new world was proving to be a bright and exciting place.

One night at supper Gregory said: "Look here, why don't we pack up and take Florence and Rod around to Klinkwan? Captain Hunter isn't likely to come in here again until he's on his way out. We could go over one day and come back the next morning."

"And supposing the boat *does* come in while we're gone?" Alec asked practically.

"There's not a chance in a hundred that it will. We'll just sit around here for another ten days or so, with the rain starting and this confounded bay getting gloomier. I tell you I've had enough of it."

"The pack is too important," Alec said. "I won't take a chance, not even one in a hundred, of missing the freighter." Alec's uncompromising sense of duty gave his words the ring of finality.

"You and your pack!" Gregory said angrily. "You'd think nothing else existed in the world. By thunder, Alec, I'm through!"

Florence looked at her brother's stormy face, knowing well how unsuited he was for this life. "It'll only be a few more days," she said. "A week at the most."

"I'm for getting the pack out at any cost," Jaimy said. "After this summer's work, my heart, body, and soul lie pickled in brine in those barrels."

But his effort at humor was lost. Greg's resentment was too bitter. To him Alec's attitude was utterly unreasonable, and now that the work was done the bay had become unbearable. As the days went by and the boat did not appear, Greg took to roaming off by himself in the woods and coming to the house only for meals. Florence did her best to restore tranquillity.

One evening at her suggestion Greg agreed to take Rod and Jaimy up the big river to fish. "They haven't been farther than the mouth of the river," she said, "and I'd be worried if they went alone. Do take them, Greg. You know the country too well to get lost."

They left in the afternoon and did not intend to return before dark. They'd row some distance up the river and leave the boat and fish from there. The day had been still, with a white haze over the sky. They took a lunch along and Rod was jubilant.

Toward evening, Alec came in from the cooper-shop and he and Florence ate supper together. Then he sat in Pa's chair in the window and read the Bible. After the dishes were put away, Florence stood in the window watching a strange light the setting sun was casting upon the hilltops across the bay. The bay itself was in shadow, the light touching only the tops of the highest hills and reflecting odd copper glints from the dark water. The copper light reached across the sky to the northward in a lurid, smoky veil. The room was growing dark, and Alec leaned toward the window, drawing his brows together as he read.

"I'll light the lamps," Florence said. "You shouldn't strain your eyes like that." She crossed the room to the lean-to where she always had the lamps filled and ready for the night. Outside, the copper glow faded suddenly and the room was in darkness when she returned with a lamp in each hand. With an exclamation, Alec jumped to his feet and went striding to the door. He opened it and stood on the steps, gazing up at the boiling black clouds moving across the sky in a solid mass.

There had been no forerunning clouds, no warning wind. The bay was as motionless and shiny as it had been, only now it was black. The cloud mass moved rapidly, rolling and boiling like coal smoke as it covered the sky. The match flame wavered as Florence lighted the lamps. She put one on the table and one on the organ, and came back to the door tense with uneasiness. Smoke spurted up around the stove lids in rings, as though someone were pumping with a bellows in the chimney. "Alec!" she called sharply, running to the door to stand beside him. There was something ominous and frightening in the sudden darkness.

"It's going to be a hummer," Alec said. "I've never seen it come so fast."

The air was filled now with a distant roar, a voluminous and foreboding sound, not yet loud enough to mute the splash of enormous raindrops falling here and there on stone and wood and leaf. As Alec hurried into the lean-to to get his oilskins, a sudden cough of wind disturbed the bay and stirred the salmonberry leaves behind the spring and the boughs of the dark trees above them. There was a sharp increase in the tempo of the heavy, falling drops.

Alec came back with his sou'wester fastened under his chin and his long oilskin coat buttoned all the way down. He carried a lighted ship's lantern. "Stay in out of this, Flossie," he commanded. "I'm going over to see that everything's made fast."

"What about the boys?" Florence called after him. But her voice was drowned as the storm charged down upon the bay, impersonal and terrible—an avalanche of wind and rain. Florence ducked back into the house and shut the door. But in the smoky room the deafening roar on the roof closed in on her with such smothering vehemence that she turned in a panic and yanked the door open again. She stood clinging to the doorknob, her heart pounding in her throat, feeling the rain splash into the room. She stared into the black storm. "Oh, Rod . . . Jaimy . . . Greg!" She said their names aloud. She saw Alec's lantern jerking about on the wharf, disappearing as he went down the ladder and showing again from the deck of the *Sea Wolf*. Somehow the lantern, showing now between the rows of piling, gave her courage. Dear, steadfast Alec, she thought. If anything *could* be done he would know how to do it. When she thought of the boys, she had little worry for Jaimy and Greg because, barring accidents, they would manage all right. But Rod would be worn out struggling through the brush, drenched to his skin in the cold, pounding rain. She thought of those dreadful days of waiting in the house in Victoria when Rod lay ill with pneumonia. There would have to be hot water and tea ready when they got home. She closed the door and followed her own grotesque shadow into the lean-to, where she lit another lamp.

She donned Gregory's oilskins and, taking two pails, went out to fight her way to the spring. The wind pushed and buffeted her over the stones, pressing her skirts and the stiff coat hard against her back and legs. In the gloom she stumbled, and stepped into the water below the spring. Finally she found the board that was there to stand on, and she dipped her pails and brought them up dripping. Going back, she leaned into the wind, feeling the sting of rain on her mouth and chin, unable to think above the noise of its thousand little hammers striking into the oilskin coat.

She stuffed wood into the stove and got the wash boiler down and emptied her pails into it. After another trip to the spring, she hung up the dripping coat and hat and brought the lamp back to the room with her. Then she looked into Alec's room and her own, searching for leaks. Rain was spurting under her window and under the front window near the organ. She shoved the instrument out into the middle of the floor and flew about laying towels along the window sills to sop up the water. In two places she put cans to catch the drips. Then she opened the oven door and put the boys' underwear and bath towels on a chair in front of it to warm. She made tea in the big pot, and when Alec came in, with his cheeks above his beard whipped to a bright red, they sat together at the table drinking the hot tea, listening to the roar of rain on the roof and waiting.

For more than an hour they sat, with Alec going occasionally to look out of the door. Florence strained to hear above the roar of the rain and tried not to notice the tightening of her nerves. Alec shook his head. "They'll have an awful time of it," he said, talking loudly so that she could hear him above the storm. He got up again and walked to the door. "It's bad," he said gloomily, "bad. Hunter'll never bring his boat in, in weather like this."

Florence made a fresh pot of tea and moved the boys' cups around the table nervously. Then the door opened and there they were, looking as though they had just been dragged out of the bay. Rod stepped into the room and stopped, the water running off of him into a pool on the floor. He was stumbling tired and the blue half-circles under his eyes looked like smudges on his pale cheeks. Gregory was behind him, his hand on Rod's shoulder. "Good going, old fellow," he said, looking anxiously over his head at Florence. "Warm him up, will you?" His own teeth were chattering and he paused before going on. "We had to fight it out all the way down the river," he said. "Rod got chilled in the boat coming back."

"We can change in the coopershop," Jaimy said, streaming water on the doorstep. He held a string of trout in one hand.

Florence had risen. "Come in here, all of you," she said, "and get those drenched clothes off. Roddy, sit here by the oven. Oh, I'm so glad you're back. Here's warm underwear." She paused to pour tea into the cups and sugar them plentifully. "I'll get Pa's bed ready for Rod while you rub them down, Alec."

"We'll be all right as soon as we're warm," Rod chattered. "It was awfully exciting." Alec already had his sodden coat off and was helping him get out of his clothes.

Gregory looked at him. "It came so quick," he said. "We hardly had time to get started back before it was black as night."

"I know," Alec said. "I never saw it come up so fast. I knew you'd have a bad time getting back."

In a little while Rod came into the bedroom in his long dry woolies. Alec had rubbed him pink while he sat with his feet in hot water. "I don't see why I have to go to bed," he said, too excited to know that he was exhausted.

"A chill can be dangerous, Roddy. You have to be careful," Florence said. "The door will be open and you can see the table from here. I'll warm a salt sack for your feet."

Jaimy, in his long underwear with a flour sack tied around his waist, was washing his hard-won trout at the sink. Alec was stringing all the wet clothing along a line in the lean-to, while Greg, in

Alec's old bathrobe, mopped up puddles and emptied the buckets they'd soaked their feet in. Florence felt that they were all together again, that whether the boat came in or not, the quarrel was forgotten.

"I'll make egg flips for all of you," she said, getting the bowl down from the shelf. "The nursing book says they're very restorative."

Jaimy turned, grinning, and she could see that his face showed long scratches where the brush had slapped against it. "Heaven knows we need restoring," he said, "but I'm going to fry these trout. I battled for 'em and I want to eat them. I'm ravenous. Man, what a night!"

"All right," Florence agreed. "Trout, but egg flips, too. Roddy, you'd like an egg flip, wouldn't you?"

"Is everybody going to have one?" Rod asked from his blankets.

"Absolutely everyone," Greg said quickly. "The egg flip's the thing."

Florence smiled at him, knowing how anxious he was lest Rod be ill from the exposure. Gregory always felt so much; he felt everything. His own longing was always being smothered and pushed down within him by the lives of those around him.

"Do sit down, Greg, and have another cup of tea. You'll all feel better when you've eaten something."

The tone of the storm changed. The steady roar had passed overhead and was gone. The wind broke up and was striking into the bay in squall after squall, separated not by lulls but by the sound of the raging creek and the rustling of the wind as it gathered its forces for the next one. They all knew that with this much wind in the bay the surf outside would be riding high and the seas breaking over the islands.

"I just don't seem to be hungry," Rod said, his eyes bright under the dark tousle of his hair. "But here, I'll take a try since everybody's having one." He sat up in bed and sipped resolutely at the egg flip.

"Wait, I'll get you a spoon," Florence said. "Sometimes if you're not hungry you can get it down a spoonful at a time."

Before they sat down to Jaimy's trout, Alec and Gregory put on their oilskins and gum boots and made an inspection of the saltery. They were concerned lest the creek, fed by two streams, would overflow its banks and wash out the piling under the warehouse. The rain was still falling in torrents, and they could hear the roar of the water. They both knew that the storm would prevent Captain Hunter from coming into the bay and they went out with their lantern, discussing ways and means of handling the problem before them.

When they came back to the house, Florence and Jaimy had the table set and the buttery trout on plates. "I suppose the old fellow—Captain Hunter, I mean—won't come at all now," Jaimy ventured. "By the time this blows over he'll be half way back to Seattle. What'll we do about that?"

"We'll try to keep from being washed into the bay. There'll be time enough to worry about shipping when the storm's over," Alec told him.

The noisy hours of the night went by, with the boys dozing and watching by turns. Rod fell into a restless sleep and then Florence went to bed. She lay in a half sleep, in a confusion of thought and dream; it was nightmarish to know that they could be trapped in this bay by a storm. At five o'clock in the morning when Alec knocked at her door she felt that she hadn't been asleep at all.

"We'll need some grub, Flossie," he said. "And Rod's awake. You'd better look at him."

"Yes, Alec," she answered. "Is everything all right?"

"The creek's over its banks. It's turned into a

torrent. We've been throwing sacks of sand around the piling for two hours. When Greg comes in, see if you can get him to lie down; he's done in and he doesn't know it."

"Yes, Alec. I'll be out in a jiffy." She lit her lamp and dressed quickly, leaving her hair in a long braid down her back.

Rod insisted that he was all right, but she could see that he was feverish and nervous. She straightened his blanket and turned his pillow cool side up. Then she made him a cup of tea with sweet milk in it. She took the salt sack out of the towel it was wrapped in and put it in the oven to heat. Then she put the oatmeal on the stove to warm up, and sliced bread for toast. She took the lamp to the lean-to and cut off slices of deer meat from the quarter hanging there. The boys would need something substantial. It was some time before she realized that the sound of the wind had stopped and it was the roar of the raging creek that she heard.

Gregory came in, pale with weariness, his gray eyes dark and shadowed. He ate little and would have returned to the saltery at once, but Florence persuaded him to lie in Alec's bunk in the hope that his presence would be soothing to Rod and make him sleep again. When she looked in the room later, her two brothers were sound asleep. Smiling, she closed the door and took time to roll up her hair.

Daylight came with a strange sulphuric light edging the churning clouds. Rain fell spasmodically and water was running into the bay from every declivity. "It'll be a wild sea outside," Alec said, as he and Jaimy sat down to their second breakfast.

"It's wild enough for me right here in the bay," Jaimy said, yawning. "Man, what a night!"

Gregory came out of the bedroom in his stocking feet. He closed the door noiselessly. "He's still asleep," he said. "Do you think he'll be all right, Florence?" He looked at her anxiously.

"The sleep is just what he needs. Don't worry, Greg. He'll be all right." She put meat and toast on a plate and poured coffee into his cup.

Jaimy went to sleep in a chair, and Alec and Gregory drank coffee and talked quietly about means of diverting the overflow of the water from the creek. Florence sat with them, leaning her elbows on the table, wondering whether she should waken Jaimy and send him off to bed. At first none of them was aware of the new noise that rose over the sound of the torrent. Then suddenly they all straightened, listening. Gregory was the first to leave the table. He made a dash for the door and opened it. Jaimy woke and jumped to his feet, not conscious at first that anything unusual was happening. "Take to the boats, men, the water's rising," he said comically, pretending he hadn't fallen asleep.

"It's a twister!" Gregory shouted. They all crowded around him in the doorway. Florence stood behind Greg, holding onto his arm with both hands, looking toward the black mass of clouds over the head of the bay.

Out of this darkness the dark wind came tearing over the hill, cutting a swath through the trees as even as a roadway. It raged into the gorge, from which the stream still roared in a white torrent. In the gorge the whirlwind twisted from its course and came howling down upon the bay. Florence opened her mouth to scream. Her throat hurt but she didn't hear the sound.

As she watched, the shack that Pete and his wife Kitty had built disappeared. The roof of the warehouse was ripped off and went flapping and whirling crazily, high in the air, to slap finally against the hill on the far side of the bay. The front of the building was torn out, leaving the two walls standing. The warehouse was swept clean of the food supplies that were in the loft and of every barrel of salmon stored there for shipping. The barrels splashed heavily off the wharf and sank slowly. Then, as suddenly as it had come, the wind was gone, leaving the saltery, with the little *Sea Wolf* made fast at its side, untouched beside the demolished warehouse.

In the quiet that followed they could hear the water again—the torrent flowing into the cove, the distant, giant roar from the big river at the head of the bay, the small voices of creeks everywhere. The bay was like a mixing bowl where all the sound was blended into the very silence itself.

With horror and fascination Florence stared at two white sacks of flour floating on the dark water. Greg ran down toward the skiff in his stocking feet, and in a second the other boys were after him. She tried to call them back but no words came out. At the head of the bay the sky lightened and the clouds broke into bunches; the rain fell in uncertain dashes and the air lost its oppressive darkness. She leaned against the house trembling and weak-kneed, as the boys rowed out and dragged the sacks of flour into the boat. Florence was breathing fast, as though she had run for a long way, as she walked across the room to Rod's door.

She opened it quietly and peeked in. He lay there in Pa's bed, sleeping as peacefully and deeply as though nothing had happened. Thankful and relieved, she went back to the table and sat down to gather her strength. She didn't know how much of the pack was lost, but that didn't seem important. The boys were all right and the worst of the storm was over. After a while she got up and put wood in the stove and gathered up the dishes for washing.

Then Jaimy came in lugging one of the sacks of flour. "I've got another one," he said. "Alec says we can save a lot of it." He went back to the skiff and brought up the other sack. "Alec says they'll be dry in the middle," he explained. "You're to scoop out all you can and put it in a dry sack. We're going to try to save some of the barrels."

The boys were out in the skiff and the seine boat with pike poles and lines, dragging as many barrels of fish out of the bay as they could reach. They worked without eating or resting. Florence opened the wet sacks of flour and removed the crust from the top. The water had soaked into the flour to a certain extent and then the wet paste had become self-sealing. She scooped diligently and carefully with a ladle, but succeeded in saving less than a sack.

Then she fixed barley soup and toast for Rod, and venison stew and beans for the boys. After dinner they went back and hauled the barrels from the beach up to the saltery, which had been left undamaged, while the warehouse a few yards from it was sagging and roofless. After supper Alec read aloud from the Book of Job while she washed the dishes. Then, instead of singing a hymn, he said a brief prayer of thanks because Rod was better and their lives had been spared.

CHAPTER 11

For a week the seas from Dixon Entrance broke over the rocks and islands at Nunez Point with unabating fury. Alec declared that because of the *Sea Wolf's* weak boiler, they would simply have to wait for calmer weather before going around to consult Pa concerning the results of the storm. The creek, having had its fling, returned to its channel again, and the boys went to work building an overflow channel in the bank on the far side. The sky remained dark and glowering; the nights turned cold, and Florence kept a box of shavings from the coopershop beside her little stove to make a quick fire each morning.

She worried a good deal about Rod, making egg flips to tempt his appetite and giving him little tasks to keep him content indoors. She made onion syrup and dosed him with it, trying to break the persistent cough that had followed his chill. Gregory devoted his evenings to Rod. They made a checker board and he started Rod whittling out the checkers, while Florence played for them and sometimes they sang. Jaimy liked the lively old Scottish ballads, and one night he buttoned his jacket around his middle and hung the whisk broom from his waist and amused them all by impersonating a Highlander.

Every night Alec read from the Bible just before they went to bed.

Toward the end of the week there came a day of cold mist and no wind, and Alec said that on the morrow they would set out for Klinkwan.

"Pack up all your things, Flossie," he said. "You and Rod will not be coming back."

Florence tousled Rod's hair and gave him a squeeze. "Roddy, we're going home. You'll get real strong again there."

"I'm all right," Rod protested. "I could stay here and work." He looked appealingly at Gregory.

"Living in this bay in the winter is like living in a well," Greg told him. "It's no good, really. There's nothing to do but move what's left of the pack out, old fellow. Pa'll take a hand in that. You'll have to be the man of the house in Klinkwan."

"If we don't get out soon," Jaimy said, "I shall become an animated sponge with arms and legs. This air is wet enough to swim in."

By nightfall the *Sea Wolf* was ready with water and wood on board. Florence had packed Rod's valise and her own things, and the boys had built a crate for the organ. The night was cold and the fire in her stove was still going when she got into bed, tired but elated, dreaming of the big, cheerful house, tea with Ma, the open sky of Klinkwan. Perhaps the Craigs would come calling.

In the night she wakened with a start, sitting straight up with pounding heart. Rod had screamed —a high, involuntary scream. She could hear him gasping and whimpering, as she ran in the dark toward his room, her arms out to guide her along the wall. Alec was up lighting a lamp. Roderick lay on his side, rigid with pain. He seemed barely able to breathe. "I'll get the fire going," Alec said.

In her nightgown, Florence knelt shivering by Rod's bed, smoothing back his hair.

"What is it, Roddy? Where does it hurt?"

"It hurts to breathe," he panted. "Oh . . . oh . . . Sister!"

Tears popped out of his eyes and he bit his lip to keep from crying out.

"Don't try to talk if it hurts. Be as calm as you can, dear. Breathe real lightly. There." She put Alec's pillows behind him and reached under them, gently rubbing his thin back. "Alec," she called, "heat a towel and bring it to put across his back. When you do that, I'll make a mustard plaster; he must have got cold in his back."

All night she and Alec worked over Roderick, and when the pain was eased and he could breathe deeply again he fell into an exhausted sleep. They made tea then and sat at the table, their faces grave in the lamplight. Later Florence dressed and sat near the open door to Rod's room. She read again Florence Nightingale's *Notes on Nursing* and tried to remember what had been done for Rod when he was so sick in the house in Victoria. She diluted tinned milk and made a custard; the remaining eggs must be saved for Rod. When Jaimy and Greg came in, she met them at the door and, out of Rod's hearing, cautioned them not to alarm him. The trip to Klinkwan was postponed.

The days that followed were full of such anxiety as Florence had never known. The wilderness, with its indifference, its merciless disregard, seemed to move in on her with an inexorable power. Each night she prayed for strength to be calm in the face of Rod's pain, for wisdom in her care of him. The boys watched him during the night, keeping the fire going continually to drive the dampness out of the house. After three days she saw that they could do no more, that Rod was not getting better. "He's awfully sick," she told the boys. "He should have a doctor. I'm frightened."

The nearest doctor was in Wrangell. "We ought to get him to the doctor right away," Gregory said urgently. "Not go to Klinkwan at all, but take him right in to Wrangell."

Alec said, "Ma should know. It isn't right not to tell them."

"But there isn't time," Greg insisted.

"I know," Alec said. "I know you're right, Greg. See here. Why can't we take him in and let Jaimy and Flossie row around to Klinkwan to tell Ma?"

"Oh, I should go along to look after Rod," Florence said.

Gregory said gently, "There's nothing you could do, Florence. It'll be rough outside in the strait.

You'd get sick in that galley. I'll look after him every minute. The thing is to get him there as fast as we can. The weather's been fairly good now for four days. You and Jaimy can wait until it's calm enough and then row to Klinkwan."

"Row out, Jaimy, at the ebb tide and catch the incoming tide around the point and you can make it in a day," Alec said, assuming that the question had been decided. "But wait until the seas go down; another quiet day may do it. Remember! Stay here and wait if the seas are high."

Too tired and unhappy to protest, Florence resigned herself to their decision. She packed Rod's clothes again and gave Greg the last of the eggs and a tin of sweet milk for egg flips. She took warm, dry blankets and sheets and made up the bunk on the *Sea Wolf* herself. Rod had grown so thin and light that it was easy for Gregory to carry him down to the skiff wrapped up in blankets like a papoose. He seemed hardly to wake or know what was happening.

Florence and Jaimy stood on the wharf in the fine rain, watching as the *Sea Wolf* steamed bravely out. They watched silently until she vanished around the point. The stillness that followed was filled with the whispering of misty rain and the flat drip from the eaves of the saltery. The familiar outlines of the bay were lost in masses of slowly heaving fog that closed in with a gray loneliness upon the little buildings. A shiver ran up the back of Florence's legs and stirred the skin of her arms. When Jaimy said, "Poor old Rod," his voice sounded unnaturally loud and she almost said, "Hush!" not realizing that she was listening—listening for some sound from behind the fog. Filled with a foreboding dread, she whispered, "Oh, Jaimy, Jaimy!" and clung to his wet coat sleeve.

Jaimy pulled his arm away. "For heaven's sake!" he said gruffly. "We should have left you in Klinkwan with the rest of the women." He turned abruptly and walked back to the cabin.

She knew that he was as lonely and anxious as she was, but it didn't brighten her dreariness to know this. Jaimy always behaved badly when he was hurt or scared. A pain, a real physical pain, settled around Florence's heart as she followed him back to the house through the rain. It was going to be so awful telling Ma; they had so much bad news. But surely Pa would find some way to get to Wrangell. If Beldon Craig heard about it he would come. Oh, he would come if he only knew!

When she got back to the house, Jaimy was walking about the room like a caged animal. His sou'wester was shoved back on his head, his hands thrust into his pants pockets; the long oilskin coat stuck stiffly out behind him like the tail feathers of a young eagle. Jaimy's face never clouded like Greg's. It jutted and scowled in a belligerent and active protest. He had an innocent expectation of good which, when thwarted, left him rudderless and angry.

Florence came in, pulling off her wet coat. Speaking more to herself than to him, she said, "Poor Jaimy."

"Oh, hush up!" he exploded, and stomped out of the house. She stood in the door, stunned by his rudeness. A moment later she heard him working fiercely on the woodpile.

She closed the door against the cold wet air and put a few more sticks into the stove. She filled the kettle and pushed it over the firebox. Then, with an armful of wood, she went to her own room and closed the door. She was so tense that her very scalp seemed stretched drum tight. When the fire was going, she had to make a tremendous effort to get at her packing, so overcome was she with a feeling of futility, an instinctive knowledge of being marooned.

When she heard Jaimy clattering in with kindling and wood, she came out to get supper and found him composed and cheerful again.

"Old Rod'll be all right when they get him to the doctor," he said, looking at her for support.

"They should have let me go with him," Florence said.

"They'll be there in the morning. What could you do that the doctor can't? As soon as they get him settled, they'll run back to Klinkwan and maybe take both you and Ma into Wrangell while Pa figures out what to do with what's left of the pack."

"I know Greg will watch him faithfully," Florence said, infected by Jaimy's optimism in spite of herself. "It will be such a relief in the morning to know that he's actually at the doctor's."

At five o'clock in the morning they got up to catch the ebbing tide. Florence packed their food in a flour sack—smoked salmon, jerky, bread and butter sandwiches, and a crock of stewed dried apricots. All the time she was doing this she was full of doubt and uneasiness. She kept feeling that something was going to happen. Now that there was action afoot Jaimy was amiable and optimistic, and there was nothing to be gained by discouraging him. But when they started down to the skiff in the darkness, with the chin straps of their sou'westers fastened and Florence's portmanteau wrapped in a piece of canvas for protection against the rain, she could play at being cheerful no longer.

"Do you think we can make it, Jaimy?" she asked. "Look how the rain is blowing."

"I don't expect it to be a picnic," Jaimy said, looking doubtfully at the dark sky. "It looks like another southeaster starting. But I'm not going to stay in this confounded bay like a pickle in a crock. There's not enough wind *yet* to stir anything up."

To Florence the little house seemed snug and protective now, but she followed Jaimy's lantern with the rain blowing through its light, and resigned her soul to the protection of Heaven. He shoved the skiff into the black water and held it as she climbed in and took her place at the forward oars. He blew out the lantern, and after a while they could guide themselves by the deeper black of the wooded hills. They rowed without talking, looking frequently into the darkness ahead of them in their effort to avoid running up on the point. Only the sound of the oars and the scrape of their coat sleeves seemed real. The wind high above them and the answering voice of the rain made Florence feel that she was caught in the edge of a nightmare, half awake but unable to cast it off entirely. Rowing in the dark, in the rain, with their burden of disaster past and imminent, they might well have been in a dream. If only they could wake up and find that none of it had happened! If only they could! But as she thought this she also thought of Rod and of telling Ma, and then only the pain in her heart was real.

They found their way around the point and started down the narrow channel between Roderick's Island and the mainland. She could smell the seaweed in the salty low-tide air, and suddenly she was remembering that summer day when they all rowed out to Greg's cutoff and the first salmon jumped in the bay. Rod had been so happy that day, sitting in the bow like a lookout. Please, God, give us all strength, she prayed silently.

As they rowed the length of the island, the outlines of the land became darker and more distant. The open sky ahead was a changing and ominous gray; there was no definite light in the east, only this changing tone in the darkness. They passed the last of the little islands before dawn and approached the Bean Island at the entrance to the bay. Now they could feel the sweep of the wind from the sea. Even in the shelter of the island the water was choppy, and they could hear the distant pounding of surf beyond it. The wind was fresh with the smell of the ocean, arrogant with the threat of the open sea. Florence struggled to keep stroke with Jaimy.

"It's blowing, all right," he said. "We'd better pull into the lee of Bean Island and wait until it gets lighter—if it's ever going to. There are lots of rocks here in the entrance, if I remember rightly."

"You wouldn't think it could be so bad out here when it's so smooth in the bay," Florence said, glad to rest on her oars. "You know, Jaimy, there's quite a wide stretch where the sea comes right in, between here and Klinkwan. Remember how far it looked the day you and Greg rowed through the cutoff? You could feel the swells the day we sailed around. It was quite a stretch."

"The *Sea Wolf* could make it in this, all right," Jaimy said, rowing just enough to keep the skiff from turning in the tide. It sloshed and slapped against the disturbed water, as the white combs of the jumpy little waves slid past in the half light. As long as there was something to do, something to work at, Jaimy was all right. "But this skiff"—he laughed—"seems to get smaller and smaller."

As they drifted into the shelter of the Bean Island, the world began to molt its darkness; feather by feather the night fell away. The water, no longer black, glinted steel and foam. Overhead the running clouds trailed light. The bay contained its darkness and the gorges between the hills were black. Florence and Jaimy, minute in this gigantic gray solitude, drifted like lost toys, exposed and vulnerable.

Shivering, Florence looked toward the narrow passage where the seas surged in between the Bean Island and Nunez Point. "It looks worse . . . in the daylight . . . doesn't it?" she faltered.

Jaimy was rowing toward Greg's cutoff and she pulled along with him, watching to keep from trapping her oars in the waves. She tried to be calm, but she wanted to scream out to Jaimy and to this merciless sea that she was scared, that she was in a very agony of fright. At intervals the foaming tips of tide-distorted waves were thrown into the skiff, and she struggled to control her oars with trembling arms. "We could go back, Jaimy," she said with growing panic, "and wait as Alec said. Once we get in the tide pull, we won't be able to turn." Her throat hurt and her voice rose in spite of her.

To her surprise, Jaimy said, "It looks pretty wild." And she knew by his voice that he, too, was afraid. "I think we should try it, Sis," he went on. "It's almost slack tide now. We oughtn't to give up without trying. I've seen pictures of chaps rowing in mountainous seas!" His voice carried a loud bravado that did not deceive his sister.

She missed a stroke and her oars crashed into his. "Oh, I'm sorry, Jaimy. I'm so scared. I don't mean to be. I can't help it." She bent to her oars again as they rowed toward the narrow passage. The wind whistled over them now, drowning out Jaimy's reply.

The seas were piling into Greg's cutoff and rising in great gray humps as they raced into the narrow passage and churned through it in white foam. The skiff was in the tide now and rode rapidly toward the passage. The first sea that hit them broke over the skiff, drenching them and leaving an inch of water sloshing over the floor boards.

"We'll have to turn. We can't make it," Jaimy shouted.

Florence yelled, "All right!" and watched his stroke.

They backed water with their port oars and pulled with all their strength to make the turn. Coming broadside to the seas, they shipped enough water to cover their ankles. Fighting the tide and the jumping, breaking waves required more than the combined strength of one man and a girl. If they were drawn into the passage they would be swamped instantly, and they dared not stop to bail. To beach the skiff was their only chance.

"Head for shore!" Jaimy yelled.

It was a matter of only a few yards but it was broadside to the seas. Florence pulled with the strength of fear. Every sea sloshed over the gunwale until the water was up to the cross seats and her short gum boots were full. She felt no discomfort but only the exultation of escape. The shore was so close. When the foundering skiff hit the rocks, she jumped out with Jaimy and hauled it to shore; she had the strength of ten as she helped him dump it.

Then suddenly she began to shiver, her teeth chattering so that she could hardly talk. "Oh, Jaimy, how shall we ever get home?"

"We'll have to watch and shove off just as the tide starts coming in. You take the bailing can and

I'll row. Going with the tide, I can handle her all right."

They watched the struggle between the tide and wind. The wind-driven seas rushed into the passage and were twisted and churned in the grip of the out-running tide. They rose in humps, curled in breakers, and parted in quick dark troughs. Then the water inside the islands became quiet except for a little surface slop stirred up by the wind. Outside, the seas came charging into the passage, rising high and breaking. Then they collapsed and spread out harmlessly on the bay side. Florence and Jaimy knew that even now they could not make it through the pass, but they *could* row back home.

They ate jerky soaked in salt water as they waited, and when slack tide came they shoved off and headed down the south channel into the bay. Florence's arms ached so that she could hardly row. Every muscle felt cramped and strained, but the rowing, painful as it was, kept her warm. "Oh, Jaimy," she said, "I was so scared. I know Ma wouldn't want us to try to go around in this weather. And even if we did get to Klinkwan and tell them about Rod and the storm, they would have to wait for the *Sea Wolf* anyway."

Now that the excitement was over Jaimy had turned taciturn and glum.

"If it's this bad now," he said, "even the *Sea Wolf* won't be able to come in in a storm."

"The weather may clear up," Florence said, wearily pulling at her oars. The full sweep of the incoming tide was with them now, and they made good time in the shelter of the islands. Then they rounded the point and once again were captive in the inner bay.

CHAPTER 12

Clouds traveled steadily into the northwest and the gray rain fell. Mist shrouded the hills, and everywhere the sound of water could be heard, dripping, splashing, flowing. In the anxiety of waiting, the gloom of the bay seeped into Florence's heart. The first day after their row out to the point she ached with weariness and spent hours in the oblivion of sleep. Then she took to cooking to fill the time, making fancy little tarts and dumplings which she and Jaimy ate with nervous appetite. Jaimy took over "old Gregory's work," and spent his hours in the coopershop. Each evening he brought in a huge armload of thick shavings to use for kindling.

On the third evening he took the organ out of its crate. "Let's have some music, Sis," he said. "This everlasting drip-drip is driving me loony. Do you suppose it's going to rain every day from now on till next June?"

Florence played and they sang. They sang loudly and with forced determination, keeping to the cheerful songs and vigorous hymns. But somehow it didn't come off; their hearts weren't in it. When they stopped, the rain was pattering on the roof and they could hear the creek rampaging down to the bay under the roofless and torn warehouse. They didn't dare to talk about Rod, so while they drank their tea to take up a little more time before going to bed, Jaimy told again how it was when the storm caught them in the woods, and Florence told how strange the sky was that night over the bay.

On the fourth day Florence's nerves were so taut that she could hardly get her breakfast down. While she tidied up the house, she kept running to the window and standing there listening for the *Sea Wolf's* whistle. The interminable rain went on blowing its drizzling curtain across the bay. But the wind was not violent. It would be rough outside, but not too rough for the *Sea Wolf*. She knew the sound of the whistle so well that she almost fancied she heard it; then she would stand by the window listening and know that she hadn't.

"They should come today. Oh, they must come today!" she said aloud, and was shocked at the sound of her own voice.

Jaimy was too restless to do any one thing. He chopped wood, fooled around in the coopershop, accomplishing little, and made two trips over to the saltery because he could see the channel into the bay better from there. At noon he went carefully over the probable route of the *Sea Wolf* as they ate their dinner.

"They'd stay a day or maybe two in Wrangell, just to see that old Rod was getting on, you know," he said. "And they'd leave Wrangell at night, so they'd have daylight to go around the point to Klinkwan."

"The *Sea Wolf*'ll roll frightfully," Florence said. "That'll slow them up a little, I suppose."

"They could lose a day any number of ways, you know. They'll likely be in tomorrow," Jaimy said, with as much conviction as he could muster.

That night they had no music. They sat in silence, Florence darning socks and Jaimy whittling; they were listening even though they knew Alec wouldn't enter the bay in the dark. After a while Florence read the Twenty-third Psalm and she went to bed feeling comforted.

The next day Jaimy put on his oilskins and chopped wood where he could watch the bay. Florence stood at the window, straining her eyes through the blowing mist until she thought she would scream aloud with anxiety. Surely Alec and Greg would have hurried back to Klinkwan to get Ma, with Rod so sick and all. Then they would come right around to get her and Jaimy. Five days—oh, five days at the outside. She could no longer fight down the dread that had been gnawing at her until her hope was almost sapped. She and Jaimy avoided each other all day, neither wishing to show the fear they both felt.

After supper Florence stood by the window, staring at the black pane. She wanted to cry, to look to someone for comfort. But Jaimy was her twin. Had it been one of the older boys it would have been different. It wouldn't be fair to cry before Jaimy. For relief, she sat down at the organ and began to play. She played as loudly as she could, tearing open the silence and drowning her fear.

Jaimy jumped to his feet. His face, so much like her own, was pale and severe with tension. "Stop that confounded noise!" he shouted. "How can we hear anything with you on that caterwauling organ?"

She got up and walked toward him, white-faced. "Jaimy Monroe, it's time for you to hush up yourself. I've been creeping around this house like a mouse for fear you'd have one of your fits of anger. Well, I can be angry, too. You aren't the only one in the Monroe family, and you aren't my boss." Her anxiety poured out of her in furious and uncontrollable words.

They quarreled long and dreadfully, and Jaimy went out to the coopershop and didn't come back when it was time to go to bed. Florence walked back and forth from the window to the stove, exhausted and shaken, humming over and over again a little lullaby that Ma used to sing. Rod is dead, she thought desolately. I couldn't be feeling this way if he had lived. She was caught miserably and helplessly in a sense of grief so overwhelming that she could think of nothing, could feel nothing but pain.

It was after midnight when she put out one of the lamps and filled the stove with wood. She closed the draughts mechanically and set the kettle on the back lid. Then she opened the oven door and drew Pa's big homemade chair up to the heat and sat down to keep her vigil. In the morning the *Sea Wolf* would come and they would tell her. She was sure they would come in the morning. As she sat with her shawl around her, her hands in her lap, the deep forgetfulness of sleep enveloped her. When the wind rose during the night and screamed under the eaves, she still slept on.

In the morning Jaimy came in, heavy-eyed and meek, and she didn't waken until he moved the stove lids to start the fire. She felt cold and so sad that she couldn't speak. He reached over and touched her shawl. "I didn't mean to be . . . so . . . so rough last night," he said and stopped, finding it too difficult to go on.

"It was my fault," Florence said quickly. She wanted to say more but she couldn't utter another word. She would cry if she did and it wasn't fair to cry. She turned her head away.

"You stay right there," Jaimy said in a carefully controlled voice. "You must be half frozen. I'll make tea." He rattled loudly at the stove and soon had the fire crackling. Then he went to her room and started a fire there in her own little stove. Florence knew that he was doing all he could to make up for the quarrel. She wanted to make up for her part of it, too.

"The heat feels good, Jaimy," she said, getting up and stretching her cramped body. She listened to the wind but said nothing about it. They sipped their tea, both of them listening to the rain and sleet slapping against the front windows. They knew that with this much wind in the bay there was heavy weather outside.

Finally Jaimy said, "We're in for it, Sis. They'll never get around the point in this hullabaloo."

She said, "I'll look over our supplies. We'll be running short if we're not careful."

Jaimy was right. They were in for it; they were in for five more weeks of it, alone and stormbound in the desolate bay. In the realization of their utter helplessness they became resigned to the practical task of keeping alive. Their supplies were low and absurdly out of proportion. They had dozens of glasses of jelly and jam, but only flour enough for one more batch of bread. They still had some jerky, but the onions and fresh meat were gone. Because they couldn't believe that they would be marooned for so long a time, they ate too recklessly the first week. They were shocked when they found that the tea was gone and there were only two small tins of sweet milk left. They ate smoked salmon until they hated the smell of it. Although they had little appetite for the monotonous food, they were hungry in an odd way all the time.

There came a day when the storm broke, a morning when the sky was a clear, hard blue and they could see the snow on the mountain tops. White frost glistened on the roofs, the logs on the beach, and the wreckage of the warehouse lying starkly against the hill. Their spirits rose, and they ate up the last of their jerky and made jokes about holding out on the fish and wild strawberry jam. For two clear days they watched the point and listened for the *Sea Wolf*. "It'll still be rough out there," Jaimy said. "But I should think Pa would try to come in. Alec knows we're short on grub."

On the third morning a blizzard of fine, wet snow was driving across the bay. The wind was up again. They believed then that the *Sea Wolf* had come to some harm, that their only hope lay in a stretch of calm weather when the seas would subside enough to permit them to row around to Klinkwan. The evening of the blizzard they talked this over quietly and unemotionally. It was their lives now against the wilderness, and they knew it.

They became gentle with one another and talked about the days at home in Victoria, recalling their friends and the things they used to do. They didn't speak of Rod or any of the family, but they talked of the big house, the Chinese cook, the stable and the horses. Florence had not touched the organ since their quarrel.

One evening Jaimy said, "You haven't played for a long time. Do let's sing *The Sea Mews*. It reminds me of Ma."

She sat at the organ and played. They sang not only *The Sea Mews* but everything they knew, while the wet snow gathered heavily on the trees and melted on the beach. They had stopped listening. Now they were waiting for the chance to get out under their own power. They sang the sad songs and the slow hymns and each night they read from the Psalms, using only one lamp because the kerosene was giving out.

The storms blew over, one after the other, with unabating violence. In the sheltered bay there were days of comparative calm, but outside the seas piled over Point Nunez and the wind screamed around the dark head of Cape Chacon. Between these two the entrance to Nichols Bay was obscure and dangerous. Some days the dark headlands would be clothed in white, and then the snow would be lashed off in wind and rain. On the rare calm days, fog and mist lay low over the islands, reaching right in to the point that protected the inner bay. The wet snow gathered on the hills and stood in patches on the beach.

One morning Jaimy took the water pail as usual and started for the spring. He was back in a moment with his eyes popping. "Wolf!" he exclaimed, and made for the gun rack.

Florence rushed to the door to pull it shut. She was in time to see the body of a great, gray timber wolf slink into the salmonberry brush back of the spring. "Oh, Jaimy, don't go out," she begged. "Shoot from the window."

"I can't get a line on him from the window. Besides, it's safe enough as long as I have the gun." He pushed past her and walked to the spring, watching. He took slow, stalking steps, his eyes rapidly searching the bushes. His hair looked very red against the snow and the freckles showed on his thin face. Florence caught up the pail and went timidly after him. When he suddenly lifted the gun and fired, she nearly fell down with shock at the noise. He fired again and then brought the rifle down in disgust. "I didn't get him," he said. "I couldn't really see him, only the bushes moving. But it'll scare him away."

He laughed when she insisted on standing by with the gun while he filled the pail. "He's as scared as we are," he said. "I'll bet he'll stay away from here after that shot." The relief of this bit of action set Jaimy to talking. He grew hopeful again and more like himself than he'd been for weeks. "You know, we shouldn't jump to conclusions," he said. "We're too gloomy. Maybe the old *Sea Wolf* popped her boiler or something. Why, I bet that's what happened! Cheer up, old girl, they'll be here yet."

This ray of hope brought a faint flush to Florence's pale cheeks. She didn't dare put the hope into words, so fearful was she of disappointment. She put their portions of smoked salmon on the table; she was poaching it now because they had got sick of its richness. They had resolved not to open one barrel of the salt salmon until they had absolutely nothing left. She put jelly in the cups and poured boiling water over it and they sat down to breakfast.

Jaimy took a mouthful and made a face. "Sister," he said, throwing out his chest in mock bravado, "your brother's going out to bring home some meat. If necessary, we'll eat that wolf."

"Oh, Jaimy, don't! You might get lost . . . or have an accident!" She looked at him with pleading eyes. "Surely the weather'll let up soon. We can hold out a little longer."

"I think it's stupid to sit here and starve on this stinking fish," he said. "I'd have gone before this but I kept thinking they'd get here. Come on, cheer up. I won't get lost. I'll just nip out and hunt around across the bay before it blows up another snow."

Florence sighed. "I guess I'm getting jumpy," she said. "But, Jaimy, let me go along with my gun and watch for wolves while you hunt."

"Look, Florence," he said patiently. "We're not play-acting. I really want some meat. Two of us crashing through the brush'll give me just that much less chance of sneaking up on a deer. And if you ask me, you haven't got the strength to climb twenty feet."

He pushed his chair back and got into an old buckskin jacket the boys had left, slipping shells into the pockets. Then he loaded the rifle. "Chin up, old girl," he grinned. "We're hungry and we're going to eat. Keep the fire going."

She watched him cross the beach with its patches

of crusted snow and pull the skiff out from its shelter under the wharf. Then she ran to the front window and watched him row across the steely, wind-ruffled water of the bay. He landed on the beach opposite their cove, and she watched him climb out and make the skiff fast to a rock. That side of the bay was exposed to the wind, and the wet snow had piled up at the edge of the forest. Jaimy labored through it, his legs sinking deeply, his gun held high. He reached up and grabbed the low branch of a cedar tree to hoist himself up the bank; then he vanished into the forest amid a shower of snow from the tree. She stood for a long time, staring at the place where he'd gone into the woods.

She was remembering how she and Jaimy had always been together; she couldn't remember ever being without Jaimy. "Oh, Ma," she whispered, "what shall I do?"

The solitude seemed to close in around her until she felt that the very trees were moving closer, and she was afraid. She went to her room and lit the shavings in her stove, stopping every now and again to listen. Then she got Ma's letter out of her glove box and read it through. "Keep a brave heart, my darling."

She put the letter in her apron pocket and made

herself a cup of jelly tea. Too nervous to sit down, she walked around the room, sipping it. It won't do to watch, not yet anyway. I'll give him an hour, one hour, then I'll look again. She glanced at the clock. It was fifteen minutes past eleven. She finished her tea. Then she swept the floor and dusted everything carefully. She paused under the big church calendar that hung on the wall. Under the month, November, she read the quotation: "So shall thy barns be filled with plenty and thy presses shall burst out with new wine." Prov. 3:10.

In the hour between twelve-fifteen and one-fifteen she washed all of Jaimy's soiled clothes, hunting around in Pa's room until she had everything. She washed them unhurriedly in the sink and strung a line behind the stove to hang them on. When she reached for the heavy pressing irons on the shelf, she was aware how loose her clothing had become. She made another cup of jelly tea. She did everything quietly, listening all the time, listening with every nerve.

She was putting the ironing board on the table when she heard the first shot. The echo was still repeating when she got to the window. Then came three more shots, rapidly, one after the other, and for a moment the echo was loud. There was another shot. When the echo died out, she could hear the wind and the drips and the voice of the creek that was the background of their silence.

Jaimy wouldn't take that many shots to kill a deer. Jaimy was a good shot. At first she wouldn't recognize the thought that kept pounding at the back of her eyeballs—he must be shooting at wolves—he must be shooting at wolves.

Once, in Victoria, she had seen a colored print in a store window. It showed a lone hunter in the Canadian woods firing into a pack of leaping, drooling wolves, their fangs bared in horrible, snarling mouths. Underneath it was written in fine, spidery script: "His Last Shot." Florence stood staring across the bay and realized that she was moaning aloud.

The days were short now. It would be dark in another hour; it must be almost dark in the woods now. She got into her coat and pulled on her gum boots. Taking a gun, she went slipping and stumbling through the melting snow crusts along the beach. She looked at the heavy seine boat and knew she could never get it into the water. She went through the gloomy saltery and out to the end of the wharf. She stared at the skiff across the bay with wide, horrified eyes.

Snow had begun to fall in scattered flakes when she saw a movement in the brush above the skiff. Then she saw him. There was Jaimy! He was struggling as he dragged his deer out of the woods and down to the skiff. Yes, there was Jaimy. She clung to the bollard to keep from falling, so great was her relief. Then she waved and waved, with funny little half-gestures. She tried to call out, "Jaimy—oh, Jaimy!" But she was only whispering.

Somehow she got back to the house and lit the lamp and put more wood on the fire. She wanted to do her part. Jaimy mustn't know how frightened she'd been. Perhaps it was a difficult shot, perhaps he'd got excited. When he beached the skiff below the house, she was able to run down and help him with the deer. "I'm so glad to see you," she said, and her voice sounded formal, as though greeting a guest.

"Jolly well glad to be here, old girl." Jaimy grinned.

She could see that he was awfully excited. He had cleaned the deer in the woods, and there was blood on his hands and they shook as he strung the deer up to the rafters of the lean-to to skin it. He dropped the liver into the sink and said, "Let's eat, Sis. I'm fainting from hunger, perishing from starvation. Meat, by George, meat!"

They'd had butter in the butter barrel with nothing to eat it on; now she put butter in the pan and sliced the liver. Jaimy told her about shooting the deer. His voice was high and nervous, and he laughed when he told her how he'd really got the buck with the first shot but didn't know it. It fell against a log and seemed to stand there as though it were still alive. He was frantic because he thought it would start running any minute. It had taken so long to find a trail; he'd only seen this one trail, and if he hadn't got the buck it would have been too dark to go on. "So I plugged the old fellow full of shells and he still stood there, so finally I plowed over to him and there he was, dead as a doornail. I thought I'd never get him over the log in that snow. Man, he was hard to drag!"

The snow fell all that night and part of the next day, but there was no wind. Then the clouds drifted away and the sky was clear at last.

CHAPTER 13

The morning after the snow a pale sun rose and sent its shafts between the hills. There was no warmth in it but there was light. The water of the bay glinted under the touch of the wandering breeze. Here and there, where the snow had slid from their branches, the dark trees stood like sentries guarding the gloom of the forest, so that even in this light the jealous, hidden eyes of the wilderness seemed to watch the little buildings on the shore.

Florence followed Jaimy out and stood on the

steps as he went, swinging the pail, to the spring. She stood looking at the strange, secret beauty of the bay. "Look, Jaimy, how shiny the water is! And the blue sky . . . and the bars of sunlight! They make me think of music. Isn't it odd they should make one think of music?" She was light-headed and giddy with relief now that the rain and gray clouds had gone at last.

"Say, you better come in and eat some breakfast," Jaimy said, stamping the snow off his feet. He put the filled pail on its shelf and came back to the door. "Say, are you all right?" he asked.

"I keep listening," she said. "We've been listening for so long, and now that it's quiet at last I keep thinking I hear the *Sea Wolf.*"

They stood together, Jaimy on the step above her, gazing across the bay where the tide-washed point reached darkly into the water below the snow. And then as if from nowhere—as if from another world—the tall white sail appeared! There it was in the channel at the end of the point! It was coming smoothly toward the cove. It was like a dream. With unbelieving eyes, they stood perfectly still, watching. As it came toward them, they couldn't believe it was real. A voice came across the water shouting, "Hullo! Hullo!" Florence heard it but she couldn't move. Then Jaimy raced past her and ran down the beach yelling, yelling until the echoes rang.

He pushed the skiff into the water and leaped in. He rowed standing up, facing the bow. Florence stood where she was, watching the sloop as the anchor splashed overboard, throwing up a shower of bright drops. She had an odd feeling around her heart and a ringing in her ears. Thoughts raced through her mind, but she stood unable to move. Beldon Craig can sail a sloop anywhere. He has sailed all around the world—he's a deep-water man. He didn't come sooner because it was impossible, but now he is here. She watched the sail billow down and then she took a deep breath. "Oh, I knew he would come," she whispered. She saw the figures of the men; there were three of them. She could recognize them without seeing their faces—Captain Craig and Beldon, and the other one was Gregory. Gregory had come, too. She watched them jump into Jaimy's skiff.

Light-headed and giddy, she started over the snow toward the dark edge of the water. "I must find out about Rod," she said aloud. She stood in the white snow waiting for the skiff to pull in, holding her left fist in her right palm, swaying a little but not knowing it.

Beldon Craig stepped out of the skiff and came toward her. She stood watching him, her face pale and serious, her eyes enormous. "Is Rod . . . ?" she faltered, as he walked toward her. She felt dizzy and reached out to him. His face was grave, his blue eyes so full of sympathy that she could see the answer to her question, but she knew she would have to hear it. "Tell me," she said, as he took her two cold hands in his. How bright—how bright is the glare of the snow! She wanted to close her eyes but she could only stare at his face.

"If I could only spare you knowing this," he said, "if I could only know it *for* you. Try to think that he has gone away . . . to a good and pleasant place . . ."

She whispered, "But I know. I've known all along. He died that first week . . . didn't he?"

She saw the sudden tears in his eyes and the effort he made to keep his lips steady. Gregory said something, but she couldn't seem to hear him. Waves of darkness were coming up from the glaring snow, wave after wave of darkness.

Then she heard Gregory's voice again, far away, but so emotional and bitter that it called her back to consciousness with a sharp urgency. Someone was chafing her hands and she got a little whiff of smelling salts. She opened her eyes. She was lying on Pa's bed and Beldon Craig was holding her hands. Jaimy, so pale with anxiety that all his freckles showed, was bending over her with the little green bottle of smelling salts. She heard Gregory's voice in the other room, harsh with resentment and so strained it was almost breaking.

"Even with this—even with this—he'll hang on to his 'new world.' What good will it do to board up this hole? He'll just open another. What if his children do die? Is no price too great to pay for the ambition of Ian Monroe?"

"Greg, Greg," Florence called weakly.

"There, there," Beldon Craig said soothingly. "Your brother is upset. He's been under a terrible strain, and so have you. Don't worry now. Time will straighten it out."

"Oh, Sis," Jaimy said, "I'm glad your eyes are open!" He dashed out and came back with a steaming cup. "And look, tea—real tea! The Craigs brought it, and bread, too." He helped her to sit up, and put the fragrant cup in her lap. "You scared me out of a year's growth, you know," he said. "If I turn out to be a dwarf, it will be your fault." He bent over her for a moment and then went quickly to the stove to help Captain Craig cook a real meal.

Silent after his outburst, Gregory stood with his back to the room, his arms folded across his chest, staring stormily out of the window. Florence sipped her tea, reviving in the comfort of friendship and love. Then she said, "Greg, please come here and talk to me, won't you?"

Gregory dragged Pa's chair near the stove and arranged her shawl across the back of it. "Sit here, Florence," he said. "You can lean back and rest better. You've got so awfully thin!"

Beldon took her teacup and she walked to the chair holding onto his arm. Greg turned away. "There's nothing left to talk about," he said. "All I want to do is get you out of this God-forsaken hole." He looked as though he hadn't eaten or slept for days. He was disheveled and unshaven, his stormy gray eyes full of pain and anger. His grief was like a child's grief and just as inconsolable—a grief against the world and against Heaven itself. She knew there was nothing she could say that would comfort him, yet she couldn't bear to have him be so unfair to Pa.

"It wasn't anybody's *fault,*" she said. "Please sit down, Gregory. Pa couldn't help what happened.

Nobody could help it. We were so scared when you didn't come. We thought you'd all got drowned. Do come and tell me what happened after you left here."

But Gregory turned and paced up and down in front of the window, staring at the floor and punching one hand into the palm of the other. Her own grief was quiet and almost numb after all the weeks of waiting and anxiety, especially after the day Jaimy went hunting. She was thankful that Greg was safe and that Jaimy had come back. "I'm so glad you came, Greg," she said.

He made no reply, but he came over and sat on the end of the bench near her. He sat looking at the floor, his hands locked together between his knees. Finally he said, in a voice so strained and low that they could hardly hear him, "We couldn't get here that first week because of the boiler. We had to repair it after the trip in to Wrangell. And then the storms set in and even Bel couldn't make it. He took the family to Wrangell from Klinkwan during that first lull, but he couldn't get in here to pick you up. Tell her what happened, Bel."

Beldon Craig said, "How about some more tea, first?" He filled their cups and put Greg's on the bench beside him. When he looked at Florence, there was so much love and admiration in his face that her pale cheeks flushed and she looked down at her teacup. "We got to Klinkwan all right. We planned to come in here for you on the way back, but when we got to the point the fog had settled down and the sea was still running high. We had to stand off the islands. It—it was pretty bad, knowing that you were waiting and not being able to go in. Then another storm broke. Your mother was very brave, in every way." He stopped, saying nothing about his own part in bringing the sloop safely through that long, perilous run.

"Did . . . did Ma get there . . . in time?" Florence asked.

"Yes," he said, keeping his voice steady. "It seemed almost as if he waited for her."

Greg broke in harshly, as if unable to bear this reference to Rod. "The Craigs made two more runs down the Strait afterwards trying to get into this infernal bay." He went on to describe how terrific the seas had been at Cape Chacon and how the fog and snow had hidden the islands and the rocks so that they couldn't approach the mouth of the bay during the lulls. Finally they had stocked the sloop with supplies and run in to McLean Arm to the north of Chacon, and there they waited for the calm.

"Did Ma get home all right?" Florence asked.

"Pa and Alec took her home in the *Sea Wolf* after we got her fixed. It was awfully rough, but if they stood well off the rocks they could make it around all right." Gregory looked into her eyes for the first time and his face softened. "Ma was wonderful," he said. "God knows where you women get your courage."

Florence leaned back and sighed. "Oh, Greg," she said, "I do want to go home. I want us to be together again."

"As soon as we've eaten we'll get your things together, and in a few hours you'll be home," Beldon Craig said. "You'll be a welcome sight, you can depend on that."

It was good to have bread and potatoes and tea with milk in it again. It was good to know that the anxiety and the desperate waiting were over. But Florence was painfully tired, and she longed for the comforting touch of Ma's hands, for the certainty of her healing words. She only half listened to Captain Craig as he told them that he would bring his schooner in and load the remainder of the salmon pack. He could take the pack to Portland where he was going to buy his own supplies for the coming year. "I'll be going out empty," he said. "Your barrels will make the ballast I need."

But when he told them that Pa intended to move out what equipment they could because he meant to abandon the saltery, Florence looked across the table at Jaimy. His face had grown thin and a sheen of down showed on his chin and upper lip, but he still looked boyish because the freckles never faded from across the ridge of his nose. Their hazel eyes, so much alike, met in silent communication. If it were true that Pa meant to abandon the Nichols Bay place, then his heart must be broken. This was Pa's new world; and it was theirs, too. Part of their own hearts had already gone into it; already they had accepted its challenge.

"I could stay here and watch the place for Pa, you know," Jaimy said.

"When we see him, we'll talk to him about it," Florence said. Then she looked around the table with challenging eyes. "We'd have been quite all right, you know," she told them, "had we been prepared with food—and all."

"You *were* all right," Beldon Craig said, "because you were prepared with courage—and all."

It was Ma who, with her love and tact, with her unassailable faith and the strength of her spirit, guided her family through that unhappy winter. Pa's grief was so silent and so terrible that it made him seem almost a stranger. He behaved outwardly in his usual way, saying the blessing before meals and the family prayer at night, but he did it all with such formality of manner and such austerity that they were filled with dismay and none of them dared to comfort him. It was Ma who persuaded him to go out on the schooner with the Craigs to do the buying for the coming year. Ma's hair had grown silvery, but her faith in divine Providence was indestructible, and her acceptance of life as it came to her was as artless and spontaneous as always. She grieved, but she found comfort; and she was able to give comfort.

For the first time in his life Ian Monroe gave over his authority. The saltery was to belong to the boys and they could run it as they pleased. They decided to move it to Hunter Bay. Hunter Bay was an inlet only a mile or two from Klinkwan on the sheltered waters of Cordova Bay. Alec and Jaimy went to Wrangell with the *Sea Wolf* and bought a little scow. During the calm weather they dismantled the Nichols Bay saltery and moved everything they could around to Hunter Bay. They brought new lumber from the mill near Howkan, and by the time winter was over and the sun had grown warm again there was a saltery, a smokehouse, a coopershop, and a shack to live in at Hunter Bay.

Gregory, after his first outburst, had grown quiet and taciturn. He neither agreed nor disagreed with anything. When Ma suggested that he take over the trading store while Pa was away, he went ahead with it because she had suggested it. But as he became acquainted with the Indians he grew to like it, and soon he was spending more time at the store and in the village than he was at home.

And so it was that Ma and Florence and Laura spent much time alone together, and the big house, in taking on its patina of living, took on that feminine quality that belongs to a home where the women are important. The whatnot began to accumulate fine samples of Indian basketry and beading, pieces of promising quartz, and the rarer specimens of Laura's seashell collection. Pressed bluebells and violets fell unexpectedly out of Pa's books. Little cotton sacks full of cedar tips hung in all the wardrobes to frighten moths, and the faint fragrance of attar of roses always met one on the stairs.

In this atmosphere of home and tranquillity Florence regained her health and spirit. She went about her household duties with energy, but she often seemed preoccupied. Laura had to call her more than once to get her attention, and sometimes Ma looked at her with concern. In the utter innocence of first love she moved in a singing world, in color and light where only the object of her love was real. He was hundreds of miles away and the gray sea lay between them, but he was more real even than Ma. His every thought must be a noble thought, his every act a true act; she seemed to exist only in her awareness of him. From the time of his departure until she saw him again she was suspended in a shining measure of time. Because she had nothing to which she could relate this experience, she felt no need to express it. It was deep and private, intensely her own.

Letters from Pa did not reach the North until after Christmas. The boys brought them out from Wrangell on the *Sea Wolf*, running all the way just ahead of a storm. There were letters concerning the business, Pa's letter to Ma, and a package and a letter from Beldon Craig to Florence.

MY DEAR MISS MONROE,

It is my pleasure to tell you that your father is in better spirits and quite well. Our trip down was fair considering the time of year. Your father has met my mother and sister here in Astoria. They are much impressed about your bravery in the North and have asked me to send a package of books which they think will brighten your winter evenings. I hope they reach you in good condition. Please give my respects to your mother and sister. I look forward with the greatest impatience to the time when I may pay my respects to you in person. I am,

Your devoted servant,

BELDON CRAIG.

DEAR MR. CRAIG,

How kind of you to write. Please thank your sister for the books. We had never seen the American Lady's book. We look at them every evening and find so many ideas that we plan to re-do some of our gowns. Ma thinks the Romances a little too worldly but they are very exciting stories. The weather is storming again but we do not mind it now because it is so pleasant here and the boys only work on the good days. Pa writes that he has gone to San Francisco and will come home on Captain Hunter's boat next month. You seem very far away when I think of the ocean but not far when I think that Pa will soon be home and you may even come before him. Please tell your sister we love the books.

With best wishes and a prayer for your safe return,

FLORENCE MONROE.

CHAPTER 14

Pa got home before the Craigs, and it took the freighter all day to unload the supplies which had to be brought to shore on the scow. The shelves of the store were stocked with more articles than had ever been seen in that country before, and the Monroe pantry and storehouse bulged with cases and tins and sacks of food. Pa was immensely pleased with the work the boys had done at Hunter Bay. He was gentler in manner and his tall figure was stooped ever so little at the shoulders, but he had regained his old enthusiasm.

Florence was too shy to ask him directly about the Craigs, but every time he spoke of his trip she listened for the mention of their name. One evening Pa said, "Captain Craig should be in any day now. His son seemed bent on stopping here on his way to their place."

Florence looked up from her embroidery at the mention of the awaited name, to find Pa's eyes upon her with what she interpreted as a significant look. She dropped her eyes quickly and made no comment.

Ma said, "I do hope they will stay. We have never repaid their kindness to us."

But when the Craigs came they stayed only a few hours, because the Captain wanted to take advantage of the favorable winds going up Clarence Strait. It was early in April and the warm spring rains had set in.

Sprouts were starting everywhere, and the trees of the forest were tipped with sticky, light green needles. The air was filled with the smell of cedar and wet earth and moss. Florence and Laura had planted a kitchen garden with the seeds Pa had brought. At the head of each row a seed package impaled on a stick announced cheerfully what to expect. At the door the rose bush was covered with tight little leaf buds cautiously awaiting the longer days. There were still patches of snow in the canyons and every creek was a freshet.

It was a rainy day and Florence stood in the window with Laura, watching Pa greet their friends on the beach. "Look," Laura said. "Young Mr. Craig's carrying something. What's he talking so much for? Why don't they come on to the house?"

"Why, Laura!" Florence said reprovingly. "They have important things to talk about."

Laura bounded into the hall and got into her coat and rubbers. "I'm going down to meet them," she announced. "First thing we know they'll be spending all the time talking on the beach and we won't have any company at all!" As she ran down the path the men started walking up toward the house.

Florence looked around the sitting room, straightened the tidies on one of the armchairs, put another stick in the stove, and then, as she heard the voices outside, she ran back to the kitchen where Ma was. She was too shy to greet him alone, but oh, it was fine to walk to the door with Ma. Ma rustled fragrantly down the hall in her garnet silk and Florence followed, bright-eyed and demure.

Laura ran in ahead, leaving the door open. She carried a big box. "This is for all of us!"

Captain Craig bowed over Ma's hand. His face was as fiercely bushy as ever and his manner just as mild. Beldon Craig's eyes were full of laughter. He unbuttoned his heavy blue jacket and there under his arm was a little red water spaniel puppy. "Mrs. Monroe, it is a pleasure to see you again," he said. And then he looked past Ma at Florence. For a moment they looked into each other's eyes and everybody seemed to be waiting. Flustered by the pause, Florence murmured, "Oh, what a darling puppy." Ma said warmly. "Welcome back to Alaska!" From the sitting room Laura squealed, "Just come and *look!*" As the older people moved into the sitting room, Pa paused and said to Florence, "Ye may accept the puppy, but mind, it is your responsibility to care for him."

"I wanted to bring a gift for you," Beldon Craig said, putting the curly, wiggling puppy in her hands. "I couldn't find anything that was good enough. Then I came across this puppy and I thought that in a country like this you might enjoy a good dog."

"Oh, he's a very darling of a puppy," Florence said. The puppy licked her chin and nuzzled his cold nose under her ear.

"I've got his papers. He's really a good dog. Do you like him?" He looked at her so earnestly that she reached out and touched his arm.

"I love him," she said. "I'll take good care of him. Oh, thank you."

He smiled and she withdrew her hand and stroked the puppy's silky head, suddenly conscious that they were alone in the hall. "He's supposed to take care of you," she heard him say.

Then Ma came with her little steps into the hall. "Florence dear, Captain Craig says they must leave almost immediately, but I've persuaded him to have a cup of tea. But we are so glad you stopped, even for a little." She beamed at Beldon. "Do sit down. We'll have tea in a jiffy."

Obediently, Florence followed Ma down the hall past the big clock to the kitchen. She felt like a person apart, very special and distinguished. He had given her a present—a very darling of a puppy for a present. She looked down at the puppy with glowing eyes and he gave a quick lick at the end of her nose.

"My goodness!" Ma said. "Won't you have to put him down if you're going to help me?"

"Oh, Ma," Florence sighed happily, "he's so sweet." She put the little fellow on the floor where he dashed about, coming to a sudden stop in front of McDuff, who glared at him from under the stove.

"Yes, dear," Ma said, pouring hot water into the teapot. "And just wait until you see the box of confections Mr. Craig brought. Laura's in a rapture about them."

When the Craigs left, Beldon looked at Florence and time seemed to stop. He said, "Keep happy. I'll count the days until I see you again."

When the door was closed Laura looked at her sister with a new interest. "Is he your beau?" she asked.

In the weeks that followed, the days lengthened and the sun grew warm. Light rains fell and the country bloomed. The rose bush put out pink-edged leaves and a new sprout, and sweet peas climbed strings under the dining room window. Florence named her spaniel Donny, taught him how to retrieve and to follow at her heels. It took a week to teach him to keep his sharp little teeth out of the tail of her skirt. On nice days Florence and Laura rowed around to Hunter Bay to picnic with the boys.

When Florence wrote to Beldon Craig, she told

him about Donny's progress, about how he got on with McDuff, and about the walks they took together, just herself and Donny. In his letters to her he asked about everything, remembered everything. Were the radishes up? Had a bud appeared yet on the rose bush? There were always questions for her to answer. He hoped she thought of him sometimes; he was her devoted servant. She kept one letter under her pillow and the others in her glove box.

With June came more clear days when the sky over Klinkwan was so blue it made her heart ache. Blossoms began to turn to berries and a hard little bud appeared on Ma's rose bush. Florence and Jaimy would be seventeen that month.

When the day came, Ma made a cake with three layers and thick white frosting. Laura bustled around importantly helping Ma, because Jaimy and Florence were free from duties and could do just as they liked. The boys came over from Hunter Bay and the house was filled with their energy. Chairs got out of place, cushions were flattened under heavy shoulders, and their voices shouted from room to room. Jaimy teased Ma until she shooed him out of the kitchen.

Florence dressed slowly, curling her front hair

around her finger until she had a cluster of ringlets on top like the ladies in the Godey's book. Then she put on her light blue morning dress and walked down to the point to gather flowers, dreamy and happy, with Donny at her heels. Above the point a spongy little meadow stretched back through the thinly scattered trees. It was dotted all over with bright purple shooting stars. Maidenhair fern grew along the brook that ran through it, and fragrant white violets bloomed under the trees at its edge. She put moss in a basket and laid the flowers upon it, walking carefully as she picked in order to avoid the marshy places.

To get back to the beach from the point, she had to go along carefully with her eyes on the ground, so as not to trip on her skirt as she climbed over the moss-covered rocks. When she got to the last descent, she paused to look out over the cove. There she saw Beldon Craig's white sloop sweeping in through the islands, its tall sail bright in the sun. Beyond, the ancient totems of the old village rose darkly to the sky.

Florence walked slowly along the beach and leaned hesitantly against a boulder. She saw the boys dash out of the house and meet the sloop's dinghy at the water's edge. What shall I say if he comes? How shall I greet him? But he won't come, of course; he'll stay with the boys.

But he was coming. He wasn't even going to the house first. He was coming to meet her first. She walked on with glowing cheeks, in a trance of joy and shyness. The air around was filled with the liquid brightness of sun on water. There was a shimmer over everything that softened edges and outlines but somehow brought out the very essence of every object. The sloop floated on the blue water of the cove lightly, as though ready to fly, while the *Sea Wolf* rested on the water like a fat duck too heavy to lift itself on the wing. The shadow of a cloud moved across the ground, delicately changing its color. The wild fragrance of sea and forest was subtly changed by the hearth smell of wood smoke.

Florence walked past the moss-covered boulders and Donny ran out in front of her with a succession of fierce barks. Beldon Craig raised his cap and came on, carrying it in his hand. "Donny," Florence commanded, "come back here! To heel, sir!" Donny came back and wiggled in behind her skirt, but he barked again as Beldon Craig approached.

"That's a *good* dog," he said, smiling. "He's right

to keep guard over his lovely lady." He stood looking at her, looking at her shining hair and her curved mouth.

"I'm glad you came on our birthday," she said.

"I would have come before, but I couldn't trust myself not to speak; and I promised your father—that was when I brought you the puppy—I promised him then that I wouldn't speak my heart until you were seventeen." He took her basket and offered her his arm. "Let's walk back to the point. There is something I must say to you . . . something that cannot wait any longer. Please do me the honor."

Florence slipped her hand through his arm and they walked in silence back toward the point. She was not aware of the rocks under her feet or the wind on her cheek; she knew only his arm and the singing in her own veins. When they reached the boulders, she stopped and disengaged her hand. His face was quite pale and his blue eyes grave.

"Please don't feel that you must give me an answer right away," he said. "I've thought of you constantly since the first moment I saw you . . . almost since the first moment I *heard* of you. In Wrangell they spoke of that beautiful young lady, and I heard there that you had gone to Nichols

Bay with your father and brothers. I thought it couldn't be true; I couldn't imagine a lovely lady living in this wilderness. It was impossible to leave Alaska until I saw you, and when I did see you I couldn't leave because you were here."

Florence gazed at him, her eyes wide with delight and surprise. "Why, I never dreamed that you would hear of *me*," she said. "But from the moment we left Seattle Beldon Craig was the name on everyone's lips. I thought you were very brave out in the rain and tide in your beautiful sloop. But . . . but when you fished me out of the bay gasping and streaming salt water—oh, I thought after that I should never see you again." She felt as though she'd known him for a long time and now they could talk about many things they had always known.

"Did you think I could ever forget your lovely hands, or your face when you looked at me and said my name?" He was looking at her with unbelieving eyes, as though he thought this could not quite be true, that only in dreams could she be like this. "Afterwards . . . each time I saw you I knew that I adored you." The light fell across his fair hair and heightened the blue of his serious eyes. "Florence," he said, pronouncing her name like a caress, "I hardly dare to ask you to promise to be my wife, but I cannot live any longer without knowing."

Florence leaned against the rough, tawny moss of the rock. Her heart, which had been fluttering like a little wild bird, seemed to have stopped altogether. She felt light, as though she were part of the opalescent light around them. Her spirit seemed to soar in rapture on the innocent wings of her own love. Then she smelled the crumpled moss and felt the hard rock behind her. She saw the tenderness in Beldon Craig's eyes as he stood before her waiting. "Yes," she whispered, "yes!"

He took both of her hands and kissed them, the fingers, the palms, the wrists. It was as if the world had turned to music: the humming air, the singing blood in her own veins, the murmur of the water.

He reached in his pocket and brought out a white velvet box. From it he took a delicate gold ring with a diamond flashing the sunlight from between its exquisite little prongs. He put the ring on her finger and kissed it. His voice became part of the singing world around her.

"When I look at you, I feel new again. As

though all my life I had been looking for you and could be nothing until I found you."

Florence gazed at the ring. Breathless and brimming with happiness, she looked at him and said his name. "Beldon Craig."

As they walked back he told her how Pa had made him promise not to ask her until she was seventeen, and that he would not consent to their marriage until she was eighteen. "But I can wait," he said. "It was not knowing that I couldn't stand. Tell me again that it's true that you love me."

As they drew near the house, Florence said, "I want to be the first to tell Ma." She ran ahead, past the rose bush with its brave new bud, up the stairs to Ma's room.

In the soft fragrance of Ma's arms, her eyes bright with tears, she cried, "Ma dear, I'm so happy—oh, I'm so happy."

In the evening she watched Beldon Craig sail away. Her world seemed full of stars and flowers, of expectancy and joy. Pa had given them his blessing and he had spoken very seriously of their engagement and their coming marriage. "It is for you to bring the Christian faith and progress to the wilderness," he said. "It's a great responsibility and a great privilege."

But for Florence, as she watched the sloop sail away, there was only the singing of her own heart; only her true love was real.

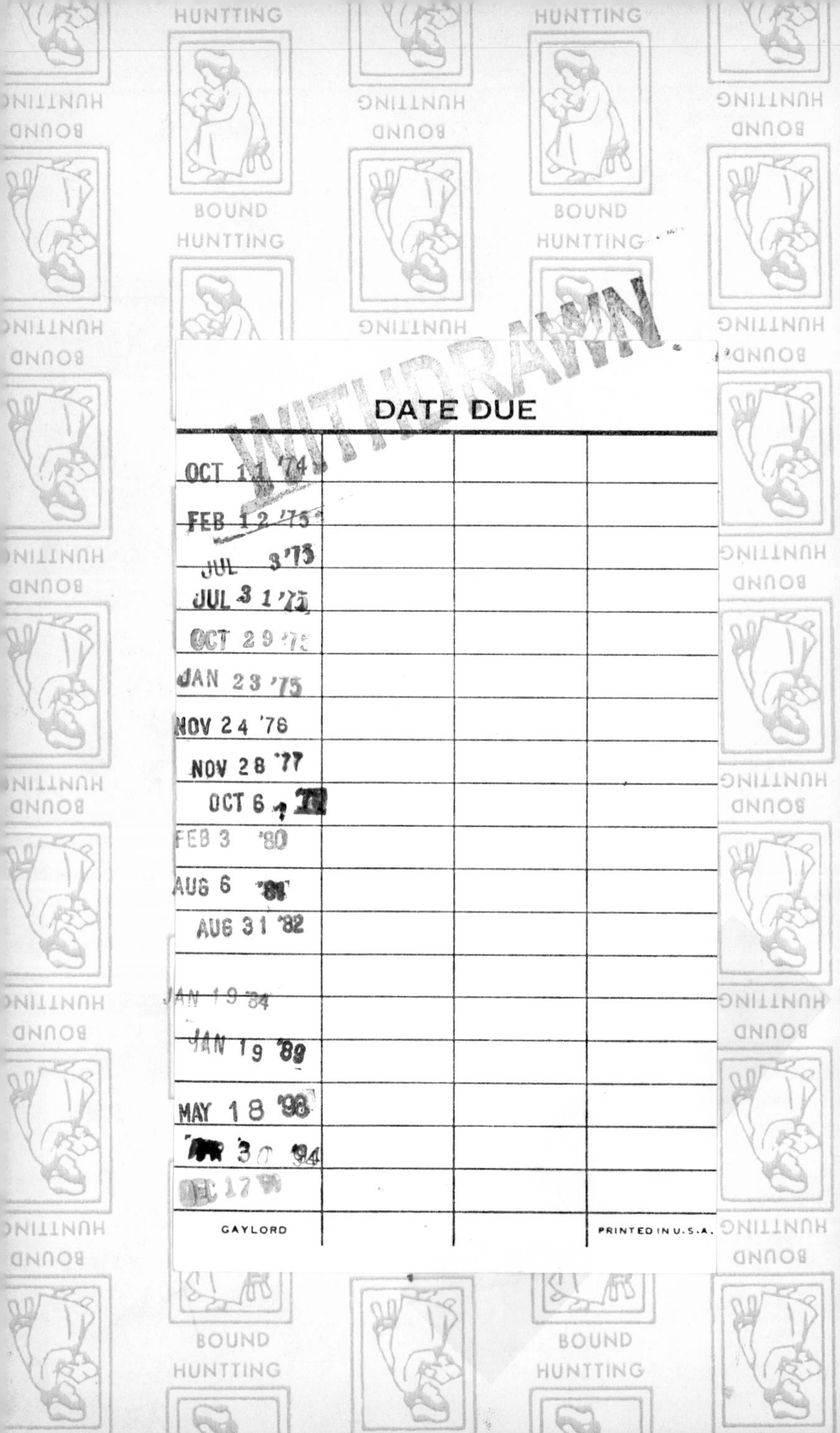
HUNTTING
BOUND
WITHDRAWN
DATE DUE
OCT 11 '74
FEB 12 '75
JUL 3 '75
JUL 31 '75
OCT 29 '75
JAN 23 '75
NOV 24 '76
NOV 28 '77
FEB 3 '80
AUG 31 '82
JAN 19 '84
MAY 18 '93
GAYLORD
PRINTED IN U.S.A.